Saladin

Piracy, Mutiny & Murder on the High Seas

Author's Note: Although many of the persons and events in this narrative are mentioned in the trial records of the condemned mutineers and in Halifax newspaper reports of the Saladin mutiny of 1844, other characters and events are purely fictional.

Nimbus Publishing Limited
PO Box 9166
Halifax, NS   B3K 5M8
(902) 455-4286

Printed and bound in Canada
Design: Margaret Issenman
Cover Illustration: David Preston Smith

Library and Archives Canada Cataloguing in Publication

Crooker, William S.

Saladin : piracy, mutiny and murder on the high seas : a historical

narrative / William Crooker with Elizabeth Peirce.

ISBN 1-55109-590-4

I. Peirce, Elizabeth, 1975- II. Title.
PS8605.R655S26 2006   C813'.6   C2006-904855-X

Canada   The Canada Council | Le Conseil des Arts
          for the Arts | du Canada

We acknowledge the financial support of the Government of Canada through the Book Publishing Industry Development Program (BPIDP) and the Canada Council, and of the Province of Nova Scotia through the Department of Tourism, Culture and Heritage for our publishing activities.

Saladin

Piracy, Mutiny & Murder on the High Seas

William Crooker with Elizabeth Peirce

NIMBUS PUBLISHING

Chapter One

Early on a crisp October morning in 1842, Captain George Field-ing left his lodgings on Tithebarn Street and briskly walked down to the docks on the river Mersey where his ship lay at anchor. Even at that early hour, the Liverpool waterfront was bustling with activity; indeed, at almost any hour of the day, one might observe crews of sweating men moving from deck to dock and back, loading or unloading the endless and predictable succession of goods for which Liverpool had become famous.

Thousands of bales of raw cotton from the United States were destined for the newly industrialized spinning factories in Manchester via the cotton brokers clustered in Liverpool, the largest cotton import market in the world. Ongoing trade in sugar, rum, and tobacco from the West Indies proved the perennial appeal of these commodities on the English market, even long after Liverpool's trade in slaves had ended. No longer did Liverpool shipwrights hammer out the dozens of "slavers"—capacious, flat-bottomed square-riggers that would be sailed down the West Coast of Africa to be filled with living cargo. Public outrage had eventually drowned out the indignation of financiers reluctant to shut down the business that had made them their fortunes. Liverpool businessmen had long ago come to the realization that the steady profits to be made from cotton grown and harvested by descendants of enslaved Africans held out less risk and entailed more financial gain than the import of new African flesh.

As the bustling town grew, wealthy merchants left their houses in the centre of town for fashionable newer homes in Liverpool's expanding suburbs. Their empty townhouses were soon filled to overcrowding with Liverpool's poor; whole families often lived in a cellar with no washing or cooking facilities, where water was obtained from a common pump on the street outside or from the nearest river.

Walking the streets near the dockyards was not an activity for the faint of heart, where layers of trodden-down horse manure mingled with the daily ordure of the neighbourhood concealed the roadbed completely. As he turned onto St. Nicholas Street, near the old parish church, Fielding saw a woman's head emerge from the cellar doors of a house that had obviously once belonged to a wealthy family, now crumbling like a shipwreck where it stood. The woman, oblivious to the presence of passersby, deftly tipped a large basket of odorous rubbish into the street a few paces ahead of Fielding, obliging him to cross to the other side. He cursed at her under his breath. He loathed slovenly women and the slums they occupied. He wished someone would touch a match to the teetering wrecks these wretches inhabited and run them out into the gutters like the rats they were.

Fielding was of the opinion that a stint on board ship was the cure for most of English society's ills—that or the workhouse. He despised the charitable institutions, churches in particular, that attempted to improve the lives of Liverpool's "cellar-dwellers." He made it an especial point to curse loudly whenever one of these pious folks crossed his path, just to be able to chuckle at their pursed lips and shocked, pitying expressions. Yes, a trip around the Horn would do the lot of them a world of good.

Approaching the waterfront, Fielding heard the cries of dock workers, a symphony of hammers on wood, and the creaks and groans of ships straining against their moorings. He breathed it all in one gulp, like a dram of whiskey. This was Fielding's world, the front lines of trade, not the fussy haggling of the customs house, a place Fielding thought better suited to squawking, silly women.

He scanned the forest of masts for the *Vitula*, his home for the next year; his keen eye soon found her. The barque was being provisioned with necessaries for a crew of fourteen on a voyage that would take them to Buenos Aires, halfway around the world. He watched as agile stevedores muscled crates filled with English earthenware pots, cooking utensils, and linen clothing onto the decks of the *Vitula*.

"Mind what you're heaving, man," he called out to a boy of no more than fourteen who had just set a crate down on deck with a heavy thud. "If I see any broken crockery when I get to Argentina, there'll be hell to pay. I know your master."

The boy blanched, then quickly dropped out of sight below a stack of crates, mingling with his fellows.

A dockside observer watching Fielding would have seen a man in his mid-thirties or early forties with a stout build and strong, decisive features. Though he had left school at an early age for the sea, Fielding's overseas education had acquainted him with enough French, Spanish, Portuguese, and Dutch to be understood in these languages, a valuable asset in a captain of an international trading vessel. Word around the docks was that he was a quarrelsome, domineering ship's master—and that he rarely returned from a voyage with the same crew he set sail with. Fielding had been captain of the *Vitula* since its construction two years previously and had commanded the ship on one other South American voyage since its christening. Now, he eagerly awaited the end of the fall hurricane season and hoped for a prosperous trading expedition, one which might entail a fearsome descent below the Tropic of Capricorn and around the southernmost tip of South America by way of Cape Horn, murderous passageway to the Pacific Ocean.

This was a route Fielding knew well. On his previous trading mission with the *Vitula*, he had put in to Montevideo, Uruguay, some

130 miles east of Buenos Aires, before continuing around the Horn towards his destination, the Peruvian island of Chincha, renowned as a haven for seabirds and their smelly but valuable deposits of guano. The journey he now contemplated would take him to many of these now-familiar haunts, and Fielding felt confident in his ability to secure top prices for the English goods he would be trading there. The cargo he carried was bulky but not terribly heavy and the *Vitula* handled well, conditions that promised a quick voyage. The time factor would be a consideration for any sailor Fielding approached to crew his vessel. The faster he could dispose of his cargo, the sooner they would all be able to return to their families in England. For Fielding, family meant only his twelve-year-old son, George, and the captain had plans for him.

On his walk back to his lodgings from the docks, Fielding gloomily contemplated his son's future. The boy was growing up too attached to his mother's apron strings, in Fielding's view; he was already showing signs of weakness and effeminacy, becoming a man his father would have lashed were he a sailor on one of his ships. It was a father's duty to cure his son of these womanish leanings, both for the boy's sake and his own. A sea captain had a certain reputation to uphold, after all.

Not that Fielding could boast much in the way of a good reputation when it came to his domestic life. His pulse still quickened when he remembered the night of George's conception in one of the cramped rooms on St. Nicholas Street that he had rented on his return from a short trip to the continent a dozen years ago. The boy's mother had served him dinner not two hours before at the Mersey Inn; he remembered the meal more clearly than the events that had followed: mutton stew after a month of salt cod, washed down by several pints of ale. He had told the teenaged girl exaggerated tales of life at sea because she was willing to listen; while he talked, she gazed at the brass buttons on his coat. It had not been difficult to convince her of his love for her and of the sexual privileges this love entailed. She was so yielding so soon that he had not even had to suggest marriage. What a welcome change from the others, fools who thought a promise from Fielding held any currency! In truth, he preferred a bit more gumption in a woman than George's mother had shown; he felt it improved the quality of sexual congress. However, when drunk, he was usually not terribly choosy.

A year later, when he returned again to the Mersey Inn after another voyage, he had asked after her, only to be told that she had quit the establishment and had not been heard from in some months. He did not guess the reason and gave the matter no further thought. He did not meet his son until three years later when the boy's mother brought young George to the customs house, where she had tracked Fielding down, looking for money. He could not deny the child's resemblance to himself; this was the only reason he acquiesced and offered her a small allowance. He felt a mixture of intense embarrassment and contempt as the customs men smiled knowingly at the boy, the woman, and Fielding, whose discomfiture was plain. It was at that moment that Fielding vowed never to let a woman get the upper hand in his affairs again.

Now, nine years later, Fielding could finally see a use for the son who had embarrassed him and had been an added expense at the beginning of his navigational career. Fielding would enlist him as ship's boy on the *Vitula* and show him the life of a sailor. Their departure time was drawing nearer.

Chapter Two

Shortly past noon, Fielding gave the order to slip the *Vitula* free of her mooring. It was the end of October, and the sky already had the ominous, lowering quality of late November. The sea had been dead calm from daybreak to around eleven o'clock, and a tug took the ship out of Liverpool Harbour while the crew unfurled the yards and yards of sail to catch the wind.

Fielding had had little trouble enlisting the sixteen men who would accompany him to Argentina—the mate was a lanky Liverpudlian of twenty-seven who had been at sea for most of his young life, while many of the other crew had served on ships commanded by acquaintances of Fielding, who had not hesitated to recommend their services.

The rest of the crew was made up of an assortment of Liverpool youth, deckhands with strong backs if not the keenest of intellects.

Standing beside the helmsman, Fielding watched the spires of the city's churches and the dome of the customs house slowly growing smaller as the *Vitula* cleared the mouth of the harbour on its course to the open sea. He drew a deep breath of the fresh sea air, so different from the acrid, sulfur-tinged fumes of Liverpool and other cities, air that had passed through too many sets of lungs. Even from this short distance away, Fielding swore he could see a grayish pall hang over the city on the Mersey, which, like many of its Midlands counterparts, seemed choked by the smoky by-product of its dark, satanic mills.

Three gulls hung suspended in the air at the ship's stern, seeming to float in the backdraft of the ship's movement, ever hopeful of a bite of food. Once, on the dock at Liverpool, Fielding had watched in horrified fascination as a gull had swallowed a small rat, catching it by the tail and hurling it into the air, its beak opened wide to catch the squirming rodent as it fell headfirst into its gullet. When Fielding was a boy, his mother had scoldingly called him a seagull for his habit of gulping down food without chewing it and for always being hungry. For this reason, the captain had always felt a kind of kinship with the ubiquitous birds that followed his ship, winter and summer.

It was just as Fielding was about to retire to his quarters for lunch that he noticed young George huddled near the forecastle, clutching the carpet bag that contained all he owned in the world, crying. Enraged, his father grabbed the boy by the upper arm and yanked him to his feet.

"What's this, then? A son of mine, weeping like a milksop? Dry your eyes before I give you something to cry about."

"Yessir," the boy blubbered, shaking from head to foot.

"You let those men see you crying like this again, I'll give orders for them to keelhaul you."

George tried to control the shaking that seized his body, to no avail.

Holding his son upright by the arm, and looking around furtively to make sure no one had had seen this spectacle, Fielding propelled him down the steep steps to his cabin, where he poured a small quantity of whiskey into a tin mug.

"Drink this," he said, holding the mug out to George, in a voice that was almost friendly.

The boy swallowed the strong liquor quickly, thankful for the kinder attention he was receiving from his father. He liked whiskey and drank it whenever he could find sixpence and a willing tavernkeeper. George was small for his age and looked about nine, though he was really twelve. Most tavern owners would not hesitate to serve a twelve-year-old, early adolescence being the time that many young men went to sea as cabin boys, but younger children were not considered far enough removed from their mother's milk to be drinking whiskey.

George's obvious familiarity with and liking for spirits pleased his father. At least in this way, the boy showed promise.

"Leave your kit here, and then join me back up on deck. I want to show you the ship."

Timidly, George asked, "Sir, am I to stay in your cabin, and not with the rest of the crew?"

His father laughed uproariously. "Lord yes! I wouldn't have you mixed up with that riffraff. They talk a lot of nonsense that'll just addle your brain. No, you eat and sleep in this cabin, with me. You're not a deckhand; you're the son of the captain. That makes you a ship's officer."

George didn't know whether to be proud or scared of living in such close proximity to his father. His mother never spoke of the man, and either cursed at her son or kept silent whenever he asked questions about him. In fact, George's first real meeting with his father in nine years had been two days ago, when the captain had turned up at the flat he and his mother shared. Fielding informed her that George would accompany him to Buenos Aires. She had protested that the lad was still in school; in fact, George had stopped going years ago, preferring to roam the bustling streets and skulk in the damp alleys of the old city. He had become a proficient pickpocket of late, his small size allowing him to squeeze in between the customers at the Leeside Market. Only once had he been caught; even then, he had only gotten a good ear-boxing from the would-be victim and a warning never to steal again, an admonition he had, of course, cheerfully ignored. Besides the money, his growing collection of pilfered items now included a handsome pocket watch, wound faithfully every day, a penknife, a snuffbox, and a miniature leather-bound copy of the New Testament, which George didn't have much use for and had planned to sell or trade before his father took him away. All of these things he carried with him in his jacket pocket like talismans; he fingered their familiar shapes nervously now in the presence of his unfamiliar father.

He remembered the abrupt leave-taking, his mother's pleas, her tearstained face bleeding where Fielding had dealt her a blow when she had stood between him and her son. The boy had tried to run past his father toward the door, but Fielding had blocked his exit, knocking him to the floor. Calmly pulling the stunned boy to his feet, Fielding had turned to his mother and said, "It's for the boy's own good. Someday you'll thank me." George felt the bruises on his upper arm where Fielding had grasped him and pushed him, squirming and dragging his heels, out into the street and toward the dockyard where the masts clustered together, close as quills on the back of a porcupine. Changing direction suddenly, Fielding had hauled him into an alley and beaten him again with his belt, "Just so you know who's master." George had crouched against the wall of the alley like a dog waiting for its whipping to be over.

Fielding's brusque voice snapped George out of this painful re-membrance.

"Why do you stare at me in such a way, boy? Have I grown another head? I told you to leave your things here and join me on deck."

Still clutching his sack, George replied in a small voice, "Please you, sir. I'd as soon stay below deck." His tears were returning and he made little attempt to hide them from his father.

"Suit yourself, then." With an expression of disgust, Fielding turned on his heel and climbed out of the cabin. He couldn't help but be put off by his son's simpering, cowed behavior, no doubt the result of an excessive mothering influence. He meant to curb this undesir-able trait in the boy on this voyage, even if it killed them both.

On deck, the second watch was busy with mid-morning tasks, already scouring the decks with abrasive holy stone to lift the in-grained dirt that had accumulated during the loading of the ship. Although a far cry from the strict, almost mechanical discipline and cleanliness enforced on ships of the Royal Navy, the organized manner in which the *Vitula's* sailors performed their daily tasks pleased Fielding mightily. With a good tailwind, he doubted not that they would reach the Azores within three weeks and the Cape Verdes Islands off the coast of Senegal before December. From that equatorial region, the crew would bid this side of the Atlantic ocean adieu, travelling westward on the trade winds until they caught sight of Cape St. Roque, the easternmost point of Brazil. But this was weeks yet in the future.

The younger members of the crew, unused to long stretches of sailing with no sign of land for weeks, began to grow anxious and uneasy. George, too, remained despondent, feeling like a prisoner on a slave ship, though of course he dared not voice his feelings. During the long days that the *Vitula* lay in the doldrums, that aptly-named zone of calms and variable winds slightly north of the equator, when the whole ship seemed immobilized by the scorching heat and op-pressive humidity, Fielding made several attempts at acquainting his son with the workings of the ship, attempts that usually resulted in sharp outbursts.

"Bow and stern, fore and aft—can't you remember simple direc-tions?"

The boy bowed his head; of course he knew these parts of a ship, but he always found himself tongue-tied in his father's formidable presence.

"Well? Speak up, what's the name of that sail there—the one over the bow?"

"The jib, sir?"

"Good man. Now point out the mainsail."

"Sir, may I be excused?"

"What for, boy?"

"Permission to use the privy, sir."

"Not the privy, you whoreson—it's the head! The *head!* Do you want to talk like a real sailor or some good-for-nothing landlubber?" Fielding looked suspicious. "Speaking of the head, you seem to spend far more time there than is proper for a seagoing man. Do ye have the heaves, or does Cookie's grub give you the flux?"

Horrified that his father had discovered his regular ploy for escaping the incessant grilling, George could not reply. Indeed, it had taken him a few days to get used to the unremitting diet of salt beef and ship's biscuit, the universal, rock-hard, often wormy ration of sailors and soldiers, but so far, thankfully, he had avoided any major digestive upsets. In fact, Henderson, the ship's cook, had taken pity on the lad in recent days, making sure he got extra skimmings of rendered gristle from the pot in which the salt beef was reconstituted with fresh water—this liquid fat helped to soften the biscuit and made it slightly more palatable. At dinner, he also gave George more than his share of grog; three parts water and one part rum with a splash of lemon juice to ward off scurvy. This was the best part of the day, as far as George was concerned, and he often kept company with Henderson in the galley of an evening in the hopes of hearing his stories and sharing a second mug of grog far more potent than that served to the ship's hands. Henderson had been on many voyages and proudly claimed to be able to make even the most dubious of meats edible.

"My last trip around the Horn," he began one evening as he peeled the potatoes that would be used in tomorrow's lobscouse, "we ran pitiful short of beef; the men looked like ghosts, and me down to my last handful of peas. We made land on one of them islands off Tierra del Fuego where no man dwells but a million birds of all kinds may be found. We caught a multitude of jackass penguins and roasted 'em over a guano fire, there being not a tree of any description on that island. You know what guano's made of, boy?"

"Bird droppings, if I remember rightly, sir."

"Right you are—and no 'sirs' necessary." He smiled at George.

"I never smelled anything so foul in all my life, but hunger makes the best sauce, as they say. We ate that mess of penguins like it was roast pheasant or suckling pig!"

George shivered.

"Are we going 'round the Horn this trip, do you think?"

"No, no, boy—of course we ain't! Your pa's business will take us only to Buenos Aires, which is this side of South America. Once he's finished disposing of goods, it's back to dear old Blighty for us."

Cheered, George began to look forward to their landing in Argentina, and their return home. He imagined his Liverpool friends' envious looks when he came to tell them of his adventures on his father's ship. How many of them could say that they'd been to the other side of the world and back?

His father's voice brought George back to the present like a bucket of cold water in the face.

"I asked you a question and I expect an answer—is something amiss with your innards? If so, it's off to the sick bay with you; I'll not have you dragging around deck like something that's been dug up. Soon the men'll be stewing and fulminating on how you brought on these cursed doldrums. Then they'll be of a mind to heave you overboard."

George couldn't tell whether his father was joking or not; sailors were a superstitious lot who believed in curses and kept odd rituals. In fact, he'd been wondering for some time if he'd be able to escape the head-shaving he'd heard was a common Royal Navy practice for their uninitiated on crossing the equator. He wasn't in the navy, he reminded himself, even though his father often made him feel as if he were.

With a choice between sick bay and a ride over the sides, George's choice was clear. In fact, he was surprised he hadn't thought of it himself as a way of ducking his father's rages. Fielding hated the sick for the same reason he hated the poor; he thought both poverty and illness were character flaws that could be overcome through sheer force of will.

"Sir, permission to report to sick bay," George said, regarding his father with a mixture of fear and distrust.

"Fine. Go—you'll do well to keep out of my sight until you're prepared to take on the duties of a sailor." He dismissed his son with an impatient wave of the hand.

George wasted no time in disappearing silently below deck like a shadow.

Chapter Three

It was daybreak when the watch stationed in the crow's nest called out "Land ho!" with excitement in his voice. The effect of his announcement on the younger members of the crew was immediate; those on the first watch dropped what they were doing, cried "Huzzah!" while they applauded wildly and slapped each other on the backs, while those who had been asleep in their hammocks below decks soon rushed up the ladder to find out what the commotion was about.

The old hands, by contrast, showed no excitement. They paused for a moment, relit their pipes, gave a nod of acknowledgement, and continued with their chores. They knew that even though land had been sighted, it would take several more weeks of painstaking navigation down the coasts of Brazil and Uruguay before the *Vitula* reached her final destination.

The second mate, who had taken the helm several hours earlier, had little experience in navigating the coastal waters off South America and sent word to the captain, who had heard the call from the crow's nest and was hastily fastening up his breeches and splashing water on his face in lieu of a proper shave.

The second mate spoke first. "I do believe we are within several miles of Cape St. Roque, sir. These waters are unfamiliar to me; shall you take the helm while I consult the charts?"

"You've had a month to look at those charts, man—what ails ye?" said Fielding gruffly.

The second mate looked embarrassed. "Indeed, sir—they were all my study in the first weeks of our journey, but I have been ill this last week and unable to give them my full attention. Now that my health is somewhat restored, it should take but a few hours to refresh my memory of them."

"I don't know that any captain has ever been cursed with such a scurvy crew as I," Fielding complained. "It's been a pest-house on this ship ever since we left port. With all the coughing and retching and the infernal rats chewing in the bilges all night long, it's a wonder I slept at all."

The second mate looked apologetic, though he knew that Fielding was given to exaggeration. There had been only two cases of ship's fever on their voyage, and these were comparatively mild cases. "With all my heart, sir, I regret that I was among the infirm. I hope I may be of better service by familiarizing myself fully with the charts, sir."

"In the navy you'd be flogged for dereliction of duty, but go on—go on then."

The second mate withdrew hastily. Like many of those onboard, he despised Fielding. It was normal to meet with a short-tempered, surly ship's captain in the run of a seagoing career, but Fielding's habit of berating his men for minor shortcomings did not endear him to his crew. Still, like many in the crew, the second mate bore a grudging admiration of Fielding's navigational skills; he seemed to have an uncanny sense of the *Vitula*'s position on the open ocean and his estimates of her latitude were usually accurate to within a couple of degrees.

Fielding knew, as he stood on deck on a cloudy afternoon six weeks later, that those couple of degrees of latitude would make the difference between arriving in Buenos Aires, or missing it by more than one hundred miles. It was useless to try to measure by the sun today; it was completely obscured by clouds. In any case, obtaining an accurate reading from the deck of a pitching ship was never easy. A brisk northeast wind had been nudging the *Vitula* away from the coastline for days; the crew was beginning to despair of ever seeing the broad opening of the Rio de la Plata, on whose shores stood Buenos Aires. That evening, though, the wind shifted, and by the morning, Fielding caught sight of the Montevideo headland, north of their destination. Not long afterwards, the *Vitula*'s sails were furled in and the crew excitedly prepared to disembark after many long weeks at sea.

The city that stretched out before them, one of the largest on the continent, was Argentina's chief port and its commercial and trading centre. Entering its expansive harbour, George tried to guess the nationalities of the many ships at anchor by their flags; he recognized Spain, France, the United States and, of course, Great Britain, but there were many others, too. He guessed that some belonged to other South American countries.

Once the *Vitula* had anchored, Fielding gave orders for a few of her crew to remain on board to guard the cargo while the rest of the men were given temporary shore leave. George was left behind with the first watch while his father sought out the city's trading houses. The boy soon became restless and it was not long before he slipped down the gangplank and onto the dock while the men played cards. Wandering about the harbour district, George found himself pushed along in a tide of vibrant humanity. All around him was the aspirated *s* and rolling *r* of the *castellano* dialect. A stray dog, thin and emaciated, approached him, pleading. George gave him the piece of stale hard tack he found in his pocket. The dog vanished.

He saw a group of dark-skinned women in scarlet and black dresses talking amongst themselves near a bustling tavern. From the way the sailors approached them and led them into the tavern, he knew they were prostitutes. Peeking in the window, George saw several couples dancing in an intimate manner that made him blush, while two guitarists furiously strummed and sang in bold, impassioned syllables. A man in a broad black hat who was engaged in chewing some kind of aromatic leaf offered George a piece, smiling dreamily. The boy hurried away from the window.

Many of the buildings surrounding the port were painted in soft, warm colours that George had never seen before: pastel pinks, warm russets, fiery oranges. He learned later that Argentines mixed their red and pink house paints with cow blood to keep out humidity and to give more vibrant colour. Further from the waterfront, George saw stately homes flanked by statuesque palm trees and broad carriage ways that sloped toward the front doors. Only the city potentates could dwell in such opulent splendour, he surmised.

It was on his walk around the city that George realized that, by his calendar, it was well into mid-winter in Liverpool, while Buenos Aires basked in the summer sunshine. It was then that he realized how far he had travelled.

While George wandered the city, his unsuspecting father pursued business with his usual forcefulness. The first two trading houses he had visited showed little interest in the goods he was offering. He was surprised by this; since the lifting of the French naval blockade three years earlier, he imagined that local traders would be clamoring for foreign goods. Since Argentina had declared its independence from Spain some twenty-five years earlier, other world powers had tried, or were in the process of trying, to fill what they considered to be a commercial void left by the Spaniards. France and Fielding's home country had their eyes on this South American prize with its rich agricultural and mineral wealth. The French seemed to have given up their colonial designs for the moment, but the British seemed eager to take their place. Perhaps that fact accounted for the distrustful looks Fielding was getting from the Argentine traders, suspicion only mildly diffused by his ability to converse with them fluently in their own language. At the end of the first day, Fielding had managed to sell only a few bolts of linen and a paltry number of cooking utensils.

"Damn the Spaniards," he cursed as he left the third trading establishment with only slightly more money in his pockets than when he had entered it. "You just can't trust 'em. One day, you'd think they were starved for bone ware; the next, you couldn't give it away."

When three days had passed with sales as dismal as the first, Fielding knew the jig was up. He had to sell his goods at list price, leaving him no room to skim. When sales were good, Fielding might sell an allotment of merchandise at twelve hundred pounds with a suggested English manufacturer list price of a thousand pounds—and pocket the difference. Unfortunately for Fielding, the traders of Buenos Aires seemed to possess an uncanny talent for judging the monetary worth of a product. Indeed, on more than one occasion, Fielding had found himself haggling to sell at market value.

After three weeks, only half of the *Vitula*'s cargo was sold. At his wit's end, Fielding knew he would have to find a more profitable port at which to unload the remaining merchandise. He already had one in mind: Valparaiso, Chile.

"Chile, sir?" The first mate, Tom Horner, gasped in disbelief, as the *Vitula* weighed anchor and followed the retreating tide out of the Rio de la Plata. Fielding had called his officers to his cabin to apprise them of his new plans. A map of South America lay spread out on the table before them.

"Yes, yes—I'm not coming home with a ship half-full," said Fielding with irritation.

"But Valparaiso's on the West Coast, sir. We'll have to go around the Horn."

"Well, that's evident, isn't it? How else do you suggest we get there? It's an eight-hundred-mile overland walk, if that's what you're proposing." Fielding jabbed at the centre of the continent on the map with his finger as though wishing to obliterate it.

Horner now spoke up.

"Sir. How do you suggest we broach the subject of an extended voyage to the men? They think we're bound for Liverpool following our sojourn in Buenos Aires."

"Ships articles, you damn fool! They all signed 'em: 'Buenos Aires or any ports such as the captain might decide.'"

Horner hesitated. "If I may be so bold, sir, your plan seems calculated to breed ill feeling among the crew. Such feeling often leads to mutinies."

Fielding rose abruptly from the table, his face flushed. "Damn you all—I'll not be dictated to by a second-rate son-of-a-whore mate who won't do his job! It's your duty to keep order on this ship. If there is but a whiff of discord among those whoreson scurvy beggars, I'll rig the ship for continuous floggings from here to Valparaiso. Do you attend me?"

"Yes sir, perfectly."

"Good—now, let me tell you what I know from experience about sailors. Of course, there'll be complaints about extending the voyage. No man looks forward to a trip around the Horn, least of all myself. But an extended voyage means more wages—and sailors love their money, same as any man. And they'll get it as soon as we dock in Valparaiso. But I don't want any bellyaching about advance wages, pitiful stories about 'mouths to feed,' or any such rubbish. You'll wait until we've cleared the bay so there won't be any temptation to swim for shore, then you'll tell them."

"All at once or individually, sir?"

"I don't care about the particulars—just do the job," snarled Fielding.

"Aye sir." The two men rose from the table and left the captain's cabin.

Outside, at a safe distance from Fielding's quarters, the young second mate Robert Marsters whistled.

"Lord in heaven! Ain't he a sonovabitch, Tom?"

"A right Tartar, aye," agreed Horner. "And he's left me with a hell of a job."

"I don't envy you," said the second mate, sympathetically.

"Will you throw me a line when the men throw me overboard, Marsters?" Horner smiled, but his face reflected his anxiety.

In the event, the first mate's fears were largely unjustified. Most of the men were not upset by the prospect of an extended voyage: the younger ones were unmarried and in the mood for adventure after three weeks of rest and recreation among the plentiful taverns and brothels of Buenos Aires, while the older ones accepted the situation as necessary to the success of the captain's venture.

While the men were told of their travel plans, Marsters was worried about their passage below Cape Horn. The seas were bound to be rough, but Fielding's insults and constant fault-finding were taking a far greater toll on morale. Since Fielding had already been around the Horn and the mate had not, the young man anticipated a descent into hell.

Adding to the mate's worries were the constant arguments that erupted among the crew over the captain's decision to pass below Cape Horn rather than through the Straits of Magellan. It seemed to be all the men talked about, though only a few of them had ever actually sailed either course.

"I'm telling you, mate, the Strait's the way to go. Cuts off a thousand mile of rough seas and who wants to get that close to the South Pole?"

"You know how long it took Magellan to get through that strait? Forty days like Noah and his ark, and the poor bastard damn near lost his ship out from under him on those wretched reefs and narrow passageways. Six weeks of twisting and turning and sucking in our breath in those infernal fogs and icy winds from the mountains to the north—no, sir. I'll take my chance with the Horn and the open sea, by God."

"Henderson said the waves at the Horn can crest at sixty feet; between that and icebergs, the ship'll break up under us and they'll find our whitening bones washed up on the shores of Antarctica—if they find them at all. And all because Fielding's not up to a bit of tricky navigation."

"Doesn't matter what you or I or any of us thinks, mate. The captain's settled on the Horn and he'll brook no arguments to the contrary. Just mention the name 'Magellan' in his presence and he flies into a fury."

The heated debates continued, with the Magellanites sadly disappointed as the *Vitula* passed by the strait's entrance, once optimistically named by Italian sailors "the Cape of the Eleven Thousand Virgins." Not a virgin was to be seen as they passed by, although there could have been that number of seabirds skimming the ocean's surface around the boat, looking for fish. Some even found refuge in the ship's rigging, allowing George an excellent view of them until men were dispatched to chase them away before they fouled the sails. George was especially taken with the largest of the birds, superb white giants that gracefully rode the air currents like ships under full sail. The cook told him that these were called albatross.

As the ship crossed deeper and deeper into southern latitudes, the sailors noticed a rapid drop in temperature. Long-abandoned greatcoats were rummaged out from trunks, and mittens had to be worn when the men were set to work chipping off the ice that now coated the ship most mornings, making its fixtures glisten like glass.

As they approached the base of the continent, Fielding seemed increasingly preoccupied with preparations for navigating the ship around the treacherous Cape Horn, a fact for which George in particular was grateful, free as he now was from his father's rages.

Strange stories continued to circulate among the crew concerning successful and unsuccessful trips around the Horn. Those who crossed from the Atlantic to the Pacific rather than the other way around had the harder time of it, and in the days of the Spanish conquest, survivors of the westward voyage wore rings in their left ears or left nipples as trophies. Those who made it confirmed the horrors of the region: two hundred days of gale per year, navigational chaos caused by the towering foamy waves that bore fierce powdered snow on their crests, nothing to eat for days but the albatross and Magellan's penguin that dwell at such an extreme southern latitude, madness and suicide among crews of exhausted sailors, whole fleets broken up and lost.

Even Fielding, who normally paid no heed to discouraging tales, was concerned, though he showed no sign of it to his men. As the seas grew rougher and the temperature steadily dropped, many of the crew began to wonder just how the captain reckoned he'd get a better deal for his goods in Valparaiso than he did in Buenos Aires. "It's a big gamble," said the older men. "Valparaiso's full of the same Spanish riffraff as Buenos Aires and a damned sight more disorganized—trade there'll be like a free-for-all—all grabbing and snatching and petty thievery. Fielding's a fool."

The first and second mates, however, were far from certain that their extended voyage would end at Valparaiso, although they voiced their suspicions only to themselves.

"You know, Tom," said Marsters one morning after breakfast, "I believe Fielding's aiming for Peru."

"What's in Peru?"

"Guano, and piles of it; Fielding would know where. I heard Myers and Company in Liverpool contracted with the Peruvian government for as much as the *Vitula* could carry her last voyage out, and Fielding made a bundle on it."

"Who would pay that kind of money for a pile of bird shit?—begging your pardon, Bob."

"Why, anyone in England with a garden or a farm—there's never been the like for fertilizer, they say."

"Don't we have our own birds that could fill the bill?"

"Not like the birds of Peru, it would seem. They're bigger and more numerous, and they're the only ones've been feeding on the fish off the west coast—not much fishing going on with all the fighting in those parts lately. It's been a feast for the birds, and the islands off the coast are uninhabited. Think about it—millions of birds emptying their bowels on a couple dozen small islands. They say the stuff is a hundred feet deep in places—thousands of tons of it, all there for the taking."

"Dirty job of loading, though, wouldn't you say, Bob?" Horner laughed.

"Damn right, but worth it when the ship docks in Liverpool. Captains can often name their price."

Horner shook his head. "The strangest things become popular commodities, I guess, and as for dirt, guano's still a damn sight cleaner than coal in my book."

"I doubt old Fielding'll be letting us in on his scheme anytime soon. I always knew he was a cussed bugger, but I didn't think him duplicitous until this morning when I woke up and said to myself, 'Sure—he's taking us to Peru!' If he don't, well, call me a damn fool and a slanderer into the bargain."

"I'll hold you to your word, Bob, but I'm certain you're right. By the way, how do the Peruvians feel about all the English ships scooping up their guano as fast as their shovels can work—do our governments have an agreement?"

"Not that I know of; the countries aren't on the best of terms these days with all the talk of European conquests and naval blockades and the rest. But I'd be very surprised if the Peruvian navy can be out on patrol regularly; I'd bet that Fielding's counting on slipping past them while their backs are turned."

"I wouldn't put it past him. All we need's a run-in with some angry Spanish-speaking navy types when the ship's riding low with bird dung. We'd never be able to outrun them."

"I don't want to end my days in some rat-hole prison in Peru, waiting for our boys in Westminster to spring us." Marsters looked out over the turbulent waters of the south Atlantic. He shivered in the stiff northerly wind. "'The mills of the gods grind slow but they grind exceeding fine.'"

"What did you say?"

"Nothing, Tom. I was just thinking aloud. Keep your ear to the ground, won't you?"

"I will indeed. Good day."

The next morning, a deckhand arrived at Fielding's cabin door with the captain's breakfast tray. He tapped softly and waited. No sound issued from within. He knocked again, a little louder this time, but again, there was no answer.

"Breakfast, sir," he called out, this time hearing a loud thump as though a heavy sack had been dropped. In a few moments, Fielding answered the door, his face a pallid greyish colour, sweat beading his forehead in spite of the Antarctic cold that permeated every quarter of his ship. With wild eyes, he stared at the startled crewman, then yelled.

"Turn her to the west, to larboard, you son of a whore. You want us to run aground in the West Indies and eat nothing but bananas and coconuts for the next six months. Damn the infernal heat here! Fit to drive a man from his senses..." He trailed off with a groan, then lurched to the side of his cabin, falling against a desk containing navigational equipment which crashed noisily to the floor.

"Sir, you are unwell. Let me call for Horner."

The frightened deckhand ran for the mate who was just finishing his own breakfast. "Tom, there's something wrong with the captain. He's pale as a sheet and talking nonsense. I think he's foaming at the mouth."

The two men hurried to the captain's cabin. Fielding was in the process of taking off his clothes.

"Water—I want water. There is no water to drink anywhere on this cursed ship. They have given me saltwater to drink; they are trying to make me mad. They plot against me and are like to mutiny. Why is there no water?"

"Some water for the captain, as quick as you can," said Horner to the deckhand, who was always glad to be free of Fielding's presence, especially in this state.

Horner placed a hand on Fielding's forehead; it was burning hot. He called for Marsters, who had been scanning the horizon with his spyglass during the changing of the watch.

Horner took Marsters aside so that Fielding wouldn't hear their conversation, in the unlikely event of a sudden return to his senses.

"Could be ship's fever, but I expect it's a return of malaria. He could have caught it years ago. I've seen men get terribly sick for days—burning up with fever and raving like madmen."

"At least it isn't catching, then," said Marsters. "I guess he won't be steering us around the Horn in this state." The two men regarded for a moment the naked, sweating captain, who had crawled back to his bunk and lay shivering on top of his blankets.

"No—you will," said Horner. "I called you in here to tell you. You will set the ship's course until the captain is back on his feet."

Marsters looked startled.

"And what if he doesn't get well, Tom? What then?"

"If it's malaria, they usually come out of it. A fortnight or so should set him up nicely. But you'll be getting us to Valparaiso." He handed Marsters the ship's log. "You'll be needing this." Marsters tucked the book under his arm. From the bunk came a loud groan of despair.

Horner smiled.

"Let him sleep. I'll have Rawlings sponge him off; the bastard took more than his share of grog last night at dinner."

Climbing back up to the deck where the second watch man held the wheel, Marsters looked over the past days' entries in the logbook. He was deeply concerned at the lack of information for the past seventy-two hours, a consequence of the thick fog and unsteady weather that had made accurate determination of latitude impossible. Fielding had set a course south, southwest—that much was clear from his last entry, dated four days previously. Without a more recent reference point, though, Marsters had no idea how close they were to land and the jagged reefs that surrounded Cape Horn.

At one o'clock in the afternoon, after several hours of agonized deliberation, he received the answer to his prayers: a thin shaft of sunlight pierced the dense cloud cover, and soon a clear patch of sky around the sun was visible. Grabbing the ship's sextant, the mate bolted for the centre of the deck where the ship was the least affected by the sideways roll of the waves and took a sun reading. From this and several subsequent readings taken during the rare sunny break, the mate established the ship's exact latitude—they were sixty-five miles north of Cape Horn.

His spirits buoyed by this vital piece of knowledge, Marsters consulted the captain's charts. He knew that the strong currents associated with the east-bound Atlantic drift made most mariners wary enough to steer far clear of the Cape itself, in spite of the increased risk of icebergs the farther south they ventured. Though it might be days before the sky was clear enough for another sun shot, Marsters decided to continue the *Vitula's* southerly course for the next three days, by the end of which time, if the winds remained strong, he estimated they would be some one hundred miles south of the Horn. At the end of that time, with or without a sun reading, he would strike a westerly course that would bring them some distance from the southern Chilean coastline.

The passage from one ocean to another proved to be as turbulent as

the crew could have predicted. During a blizzard that lasted the better part of a week, wave after massive wave pounded over the decks
of the *Vitula*, spilling freezing seawater down the hatches into the
men's sleeping quarters. The men spent the greater part of each day
manning the bilge pumps in the all-consuming effort to keep their
ship afloat. No one slept or ate much; at all times of the day and
night, the men prayed aloud for deliverance. Marsters struggled to
keep his precious charts and logbook dry, wrapping them in layers
of burlap and covering them with his own oilcloth. He and Horner
took turns on the pitching deck, making sure the reefed sails were not
blowing out of the yards and were holding *Vitula* into the wind.

Confined to his cabin, the sick captain kept pace with the storm,
matching it howl for howl in his delirious state. Then, almost at the
same time as the storm abated, the illness seemed to loosen its grip
on Fielding and his fever broke. His fitful periods of unconscious-
ness were replaced with normal sleep, and a return to full health
seemed imminent. Some of the crew seemed relieved by the news
while others grumbled amongst themselves that they would be far
better off without him.

For days, the crew had been subsisting on a meagre diet of salt beef
and ship's biscuit, but now even these staples were in short supply.
As their appetites returned with the calmer weather, the men were
soon shooting at the storm-exhausted albatross in the rigging rather
than shooing them away, much to George's chagrin.

"Never you mind, my dear," said the cook as he busied himself
plucking feathers from the breast of an especially plump specimen,
the ship rocking violently beneath their feet. "You'll forget you was
ever sad when you taste this feller well roasted and served underneath
the sauce I'm about to make."

Several of the men were in favor of making land and reprovisioning the ship with Magellan's penguin to see them through the next
leg of their journey up the Chilean coast, but Marsters calculated

that with favorable winds, they would be able to make Valparaiso on short rations.

As the ship began its northward climb along the Chilean coastline, the temperature and the spirits of the crew began to rise. Heavy woolen sweaters, socks, and mittens were washed and hung to dry along makeshift clotheslines on the deck of the *Vitula*, and the more forward-looking of the men even brought out their darning needles to repair the holes that had appeared in their clothing during the voyage. Fielding, still a convalescent, sat wrapped in blankets on deck in good weather, too weak to give many orders, but nevertheless quick to point out the men's deficiencies as they worked about him.

Sneaking peeks through his father's spyglass, George saw the coastline of southern Chile beginning to take shape as they drew closer to their destination. He saw dense forests interspersed with plains where cattle grazed and distant mountains that Marsters told him belonged to the Andes chain. Some of these mountains showed signs of volcanic activity, their crests hollowed out and blackened like chimney tops. There were many small islands just off the coast where colonies of birds nested in relative safety. Drawing closer to land, George could see that the Chilean coastline was a maze of fjords, gorges and inlets; a majestic and forbidding landscape whose face changed with the seismic activity simmering beneath its surface. On November 19, 1822, a major earthquake off this coast set in motion three tsunamis that devastated the port of Valparaiso, taking most of its public buildings, churches and seven hundred homes. Some twenty years later, the city had largely recovered from this disastrous blow from the sea, though as the *Vitula* drew nearer to the port, the crew could see that parts of the city still had the look of ongoing construction projects.

The first order of business was docking the ship. *Vitula* joined the large number of ships at anchor in the spacious harbour. One contingent of the crew dropped anchor while another lowered a longboat down the side of the *Vitula* and commenced rowing for shore. The captain, now more or less fully restored to health, jumped out on the sandy beach as the crew shipped oars, scanning the waterfront for likely-looking trading houses. His eye ran over the familiar assortment of decrepit-looking warehouses and drinking and gambling establishments interspersed with bawdy houses, sights to charm a sailor's eye. It was the same in any port one visited anywhere in the world, Fielding reflected. He knew from his previous excursions that the place to do business in Valparaiso was at Customs Square in the heart of the city, and he knew how to get there. He would have a drink at La Nave tavern near the square, leaving the men to explore the seedy taverns of the waterfront while he conducted his business. Not that he cared anymore what price he might get for the ship's cargo. His main goal was to dump the merchandise here to make room for the tonnes of guano he was indeed planning on loading in further up the coast. This stop was merely a refreshment before the real games could begin.

Chapter Four

On board the *Vitula*, the air rang with the sounds of continuous hammering. The ship's carpenter and a work party of ten were building bulwarks and shifting boards out of wood purchased in Valparaiso to carry the piles of guano soon to be loaded. The men worked in silence, their faces rigid with concentration and anger. Every now and then, one would pause to wipe the sweat from his brow, shake his head, and mumble "That bastard!" in tones of disbelief.

Only two days earlier, when their ship had weighed anchor and cleared the mouth of Valparaiso Bay, had Fielding informed the men of his plan to continue up the coast to Peru and to load up on its rich bounty. Horner and Marsters had looked at each other with raised eyebrows; neither was surprised at this turn of events.

"And how far away might Peru be, sir?" one of the men had asked.

"About a week, if the weather's good," said Fielding in a reproachful tone. He hated being questioned by inferiors, and on this ship, everyone was an inferior.

"Ain't it more like a thousand miles away, sir?" asked an exasperated voice from the back of a group of men on deck.

"Who said that? Damn you! Are you questioning my authority?" yelled Fielding. "I know this coast like the back of my hand. I've been to Peru and back and made good money—which is a helluva lot more than I can say for you sorry lot."

"Where exactly in Peru are we headed sir? A big country, ain't it?"

"The island of Chincha's the place. If we're lucky, we'll never have to set foot on the mainland. I've had my fill of Spaniards."

From the looks on the faces of the men, it seemed they felt the same about Fielding.

Later that day, having been curtly relieved of his navigational duties by the captain, Marsters passed the time by studying the charts. The town nearest Chincha on the Peruvian mainland appeared to be Pisco, while Callao, seaport of the Peruvian capital, Lima, was about one hundred and forty miles north. With the tradewinds blowing southeast along the Chilean–Peruvian coast, getting to Chincha would be fairly quick, taking somewhere between a week to ten days, but the return voyage south would be much longer. Hauling by the wind on port tack for hundreds of miles back down the coast, the *Vitula* could be well over three weeks returning to Valparaiso, where she would surely need a refit after so many weeks at sea before renegotiating the Horn and the Atlantic crossing. With such a duplicitous and volatile captain at the helm, the mate guessed there would be defections when they made land in Chile again; some of the men were fed up and ready to take their chances on another ship heading back to England under a more congenial helmsman.

Marsters was interrupted in his deliberations by George's cry from above deck.

"Whale! I saw him just now!"

Several of the crew rushed to the side of the ship where the boy was excitedly pointing. They could clearly make out the whale's huge shape as it swam just beneath the surface of the water alongside them. George thrilled to the sight of the great beast breaking the surface to breathe, and the geyser-like spray of water that it emitted from its blowhole before diving down again. One of the men who had served on a Gloucester whaler in his youth surmised that this was a sperm whale, the species common to south Pacific waters and prized for its ambergris, used in the manufacture of perfume. Several of the men cursed their luck at not having along an experienced harpooner to bag this fellow, "for his oil must be as good as guano."

On the day the island of Chincha was finally sighted, Fielding gave the order to drop anchor at a point about five hundred yards from the shoreline—a short trip for the rowers of the longboats that would transport the guano back to the waiting *Vitula*. From a chest in his cabin, Fielding removed the store of firearms he had kept locked away during the voyage. He didn't want any damn Spaniards digging too deeply into his affairs. He knew that the waters around Chincha were teeming with pirates of all nationalities, eager to save themselves the work of scooping up guano by boarding someone else's loaded ship. Fielding vowed he would not be a victim of piracy.

As soon as the work party made land on the island, their nostrils were assailed with an overpowering stench of rotten fish while their ears rang with the screeching of seabirds upset at being disturbed. The strong sun and the birds' droppings had bleached the landscape, which seemed to radiate heat and putrefaction. Several of the men vomited, their senses overwhelmed.

Fielding urged them on—even taking his turn with the shovel for a few hours. He was as anxious as the rest of the men to get the ship loaded and to weigh anchor for home; nine months had elapsed since they'd left Liverpool, and the captain had no desire to prolong his ship's stay in unfriendly waters.

After four days of labour in hellish conditions, the *Vitula* was finally loaded. Fielding had posted a lookout party on board while the guano was being collected, keeping his own spyglass near at hand at all times and frequently scanning the horizon for ships.

It was purely by chance that the captain of a small fishing boat, bringing its catch into Pisco, was overheard at dockside by a Peruvian navy official telling his friend about an impressive-looking barque he had seen at anchor off Chincha the previous afternoon. He had not been able to ascertain the ship's nationality; Fielding had at least been clever enough to lower the Union Jack before the pillaging began. With no ships scheduled to take on guano that week, the official quickly boarded a navy schooner in the company of fifty soldiers of the Peruvian government and made for the island. Too many foreigners had been making off with valuable Peruvian property lately, and the government was eager to catch someone in the act and make an example of him. The schooner's captain, aware that the crew of the offending vessel would be on a sharp lookout for ships in the vicinity, was careful to keep the island between his ship and the *Vitula*. The last thing he wanted was a sea chase, though he was sure his swift schooner could easily outpace the heavily loaded barque.

The Peruvians dropped anchor on Chincha's far shore and disembarked, safely out of view of the *Vitula*'s crew, who, having completed their onerous work, were now enjoying their midday meal. The navy official was disappointed—he had hoped to catch the foreigners on the beach red-handed. He would have to change tack and board the vessel in order to make his arrests. "Man the longboat, men!" he shouted. "We'll nab them on their own ship." At his command, experienced oarsmen took their places on the benches, and with easy strokes on the light sea, they were soon within hailing distance of the *Vitula*.

"In the name of the government of Peru, I command you to drop your weapons and prepare to be boarded!" the navy official shouted in Spanish when the longboat was within a few yards of the *Vitula*.

Fielding, who had been relaxing over a mug of grog in his cabin, clambered to the deck, hauling a pistol out of his jacket pocket as he ran. He waved his arms frantically in the direction of the approaching longboat and called to all those on deck.

"Marsters! Cut the hawser! We're being boarded! Haul up the sails—make haste, you ruffians, or it's a Spanish prison for us all!"

As he gave these orders, the longboat's rowers closed the gap between the Peruvian government and its prize, and oars were already being shipped and grappling hooks made fast to the *Vitula's* railing.

"Men! To your weapons! Shoot—shoot, damn you!" Fielding screamed, firing wildly at the nearest Peruvian soldier who was now levering himself aboard the *Vitula.* Fielding's aim was off and the bullet missed the soldier by several feet. Regaining his footing, the soldier returned fire, and a bullet tore through Fielding's right shoulder, sending him reeling backward from the impact. His pistol clattered to the deck.

Seeing that the mates and the rest of the crew were unarmed and making no moves toward defending their captain, the soldiers held their fire. The crew scattered like frightened mice for the safety of their quarters with the Peruvians hot on their heels.

One gallant soldier, cognizant of the courtesy to be accorded a ship's captain, escorted the half-conscious Fielding to his cabin and helped him to change into a clean shirt and jacket—a futile gesture as blood continued to pour out of Fielding's shoulder wound, soaking through his clothes.

The captain and his men disembarked at gunpoint and loaded in stages into the longboat that transported them to the government schooner bound for Pisco. A contingent of Peruvian soldiers took command of the *Vitula,* hoisting the red-and-white flag of Peru to the peak of the mizzen mast, and weighing anchor to follow the schooner's lead on the fourteen-mile journey to the mainland. Seabirds swooped and dove around the two ships, glad to be rid of human interference on their island for the time being.

The army commander at Pisco who placed Fielding officially under arrest gave orders that the wounded man be taken to the hospital of the sisters of charity, where his wound could be dressed. Word of the capture of a British vessel had obviously preceded the official arrest, and a crowd of Piscoans were already gathered at the dock to see what would happen next. They saw the British captain, who could neither walk nor stand, so weak was he from loss of blood, mounted on a mule and supported on each side by soldiers, making his slow and painful exit from the dockside. In his weakened state, Fielding had a vague feeling of being in a dream, a familiar yet altered story. By the time the slow procession had arrived at the nursing convent, Fielding had remembered what the story was: Jesus' entry into Jerusalem mounted on a donkey—the first Palm Sunday. That procession had been triumphant; Fielding's, shameful. No crowds cheered him on his way. He was met with silence.

Whispering amongst themselves, the sisters at the convent hospital expertly dressed Fielding's wound using bandages that had been bleached and made sterile in the hot sun; they had tended many such injuries during this turbulent period of their country's history, although their daily prayers were for peace. The ball had passed cleanly through Fielding's shoulder, leaving the lungs and major arteries untouched. The captain was, indeed, a lucky man. With no sign of infection setting in, the nuns told the commander that their patient was on the mend.

Military officials were notified and Fielding was removed to the *Vitula*, now the property of the Peruvian government. Along with his crew, he was placed under heavy guard. The English sailors and their stolen prize embarked for Callao, some one hundred and forty miles to the north. The war schooner that had surprised them now followed them up the coast, making sure there were no unexpected detours. In the late afternoon, the two vessels dropped anchor in a sheltered inlet and the *Vitula*'s men were discharged of their duties. Their quarters below deck were now a prison, where they slept guarded by a small band of Peruvian soldiers. Shortly before dawn, the men were awoken by a sharp, off-key bugle blast and were herded back on deck to make ready the sails for the next leg of their journey. In this fashion, the *Vitula* was escorted to Callao.

As the ships approached the port, the *Vitula's* men saw a little town almost dwarfed by two heavily fortified castles in the Moorish style and by a fort at the water's edge, with twenty mounted guns pointing straight at them—not a sight calculated to put foreign prisoners at ease. Callao was clearly a military town; it was the Pacific station of the American navy and was best known for its military prison, as the men were about to discover.

As the two boats made anchor in Callao Harbour, George, who had been huddling below deck for most of the last voyage, terrified at the turn of events, ventured onto the deck and saw several frigates docked in the immediate vicinity flying the American stars and stripes. Though the war of 1812 was long over, many British sailors still regarded the flag of their former colony with frank distrust. "Damn Yankees," George heard spat out under the breath of one of the crew, spying the American ships at anchor. "Dunno which is worse—them or the Spaniards."

"*Silencio!*" bellowed the guard on duty in George's direction, making him jump, then bristle.

"You heard him, boy. Shut your trap," laughed the English crewman softly.

Why was everybody always yelling at him? As far as nationalities went, George was inclined to believe that the British were just as bad as Spaniards for cussedness.

The soldiers lost no time in disembarking the men and marching them straight into prison. Fielding, disembarked last, remained a silent observer of the whole procedure. Since his ship's capture, Fielding had barely spoken two words to anyone—but his silence was canny. He had listened to his captors talking outside his cabin on their trip up the coast, quite familiar with their language, yet cleverly adept at concealing the fact.

Now, after he was escorted to a private cell in one of the castle-like fortresses and interrogated, he continued the act, giving his captors to understand through a few words and gestures that a great mistake had been made; he hadn't been stealing. His employers, Myers and Company, had an arrangement with their country—he was simply following instructions. When asked why he had fired at the soldier, Fielding made gestures indicating that he had thought the captors were bandits masquerading as soldiers, attempting to board his ship illegally.

The interrogators left Fielding's cell and spoke quietly amongst themselves. The story, as far as they were able to understand it, seemed plausible. The Peruvians did not want trouble from the British, a world power with a navy that could easily crush theirs and ruin their trade. They decided to send word to Myers in England to see if they could corroborate Fielding's story. While they waited for a reply, and with some misgivings, Fielding was released on parole. He was allowed to go about town unsupervised, on the condition that he not try to take command of the *Vitula* until his statement was confirmed and the necessary guano fees paid. A board of inquiry concluded that the crew of the unfortunate ship was not guilty; they had offered no resistance when their ship was boarded, and they were released on good behavior after nine days' imprisonment. Most were extremely thankful to have parted company with Fielding and his sorry business.

At loose ends now that they were freed, Fielding and his son wandered the streets of Callao and acquainted themselves with its affairs. They weren't long in discovering that there were only two places to stay in town: the Marine Hotel, where naval officers and midshipmen put up when on shore leave, and "Davy Howells," where the merchant set stayed. Mr. Howells, a mild and servile man, put the Fieldings up in his smallest and dirtiest room, given their straitened circumstances. As they trundled down the three flights of stairs to the ground floor the next morning, they could hear the magisterial voice of Mr. Howells' imposing Spanish wife, browbeating a client who had not paid his last night's rent. Her voluminous bosom heaved with outrage as she demanded, in broken English, how the transgressor expected her to feed her family. "How I feed my little ones?" (She and her husband were childless.) "How I keep rooms clean you don't pay?" Clearly, one did not cross Esmerelda Howells with impunity.

Fielding's several nighttime excursions soon apprised him of his chances for escape from Callao. The place was crawling with sailors of all stripes, naval and mercantile; besides a few thread-and-needle stores, most of the town's business centred around catering to their needs, especially for liquor. It was at one such grog shop that Fielding made his first approach to a suitably desperate-looking sailor.

"Bartender, pour us two glasses of whiskey, if you please," he called out to the tavern keeper in commanding Spanish.

"Si, senor," the bartender smiled, revealing a dazzling gold-capped front tooth as he poured the liquor.

Fielding pushed one glass in front of the sailor, who stared at Fielding in silence.

"Ola, amigo," he began in a friendly tone, but the man detected his English accent and quickly moved to another stool.

Fielding found that a similar situation held for all the sailors he approached, even those to whom he first held out a handful of coins. Of course, many of them had heard of Fielding's case and knew what he would propose even before he asked. None was willing to take the risk of capture by helping him cut the *Vitula* free and sail her away, even under cover of darkness.

Returning back to Howells' Hotel one evening with nothing to show for his efforts but rejections, a discouraged Fielding climbed the stairs to his room and found his door unlocked. *Must be the boy out rummaging up something to eat,* he reflected. *He never thinks to lock the door.* Taking off his jacket and throwing it on the floor,

Fielding crossed the room in the darkness, too tired to light a candle. As he was about to lie down on his cot for the night, a pair of hands grabbed him by the wrists, pinning his hands firmly behind his back.

"Captain Fielding, you are under arrest for violating the conditions of your parole and seeking to illegally take command of the ship *Vitula*. You have solicited help in your illegal enterprise from Peruvian sailors." The heavily accented voice of the policeman accompanied the binding of Fielding's hands behind him. Circling his prisoner and shaking his head in mild disappointment, the officer paused in front of the captain.

"My dear Fielding, did you really think we were so stupid as to let you go unwatched?" He smiled broadly, showing off a gold-plated front tooth.

The prison where Fielding was incarcerated was filled with the drunk, disorderly, and indebted of Callao. It smelled of urine and stale cigar smoke. Horses and mules were boarded in stalls next to the prisoners' cells, and some of the prisoners who had made friends with the guards were free to borrow the animals to keep occasional appointments outside the prison, provided they returned before sundown. Most of them did, finding the fraternal spirit that prevailed at the jail to their liking, even if the accommodations were rather spartan. Friends and relatives came to visit, and in the evenings, one could not find a better place for cards and dice than the Callao jail.

George came to visit his father every day. Fielding was now the only other English-speaking person he knew in the town, the *Vitula* crew having scattered like autumn leaves in a windstorm shortly after their acquittals. He almost felt sorry for his father as he sat, day after day, alone in his cell. George was frightened about what the Peruvians were likely to do to Fielding. He knew that his father's violation of the terms of his parole made the Peruvians less likely to believe that the guano caper had been a misunderstanding, and more likely to convict him of theft. His attempted shooting of a soldier made him a dangerous criminal. Whether they chose to hang Fielding or let him rot in prison, George knew his own chances of seeing home again were growing slimmer by the day.

Fielding sensed his son's terror and was repulsed by it. The lad was a complete failure, he saw that plainly now. Soon, though, Fielding saw how he could use George's fear of never getting home to his advantage.

"Say, lad," he said confidingly to the boy one evening while the guards were engaged in their nightly game of poker. "How'd you like to spring me from this hell-hole?"

George looked at his father through the cell bars incredulously. "Me, sir?"

"Who else?"

"Sir, I don't want any more trouble from the Spaniards."

Quelling for a moment his anger at this treachery, Fielding asked, "How've you been getting by since the bastards got me?"

George flushed. He had, in fact, been back at his old trick of picking pockets on the waterfront and had been keeping clear of Esmerelda Howells' wrath by dutifully paying his dues at the hotel with the proceeds.

"Mr. Howells said I could stay if I minded the horses for him and scrubbed pots in the kitchen after supper," he lied.

"And you think you'll clear enough to buy your passage back to England, do you?"

George said nothing.

"I've got news for you, boy. You and I ain't getting out of this god-forsaken country unless you spring me, and that's the plain truth of the matter. So unless you want to die among raving papists and whatever miserable rabid-dog Yankee scum that washes up on these stinking shores, you'll make up your mind to help me get out of this pit."

George had a sudden impulse to flee, to leave his father to his fate. In his heart he felt that Fielding deserved hanging, and he hated the way his father was trying to involve him in a mess that he, Fielding, had created. With his father's words still ringing in his ears, the boy vanished into the gathering dusk. Fielding was lulled to sleep by a raucous chorus of voices led by the on-duty guard as the evening card players cheerfully cursed at each other.

A day passed with no visit from George. Fielding brooded, wondering if he'd finally pushed the lad too far. He couldn't sleep that night.

Early the next morning, George slipped into the jail like a ghost and dropped the key to Fielding's cell in his sleepless father's hand, then quickly exited the building before the sleeping guard discovered his theft. He didn't want to be the one to release his father, though he had provided the instrument for his escape.

It was in the evening that the fugitive made his surreptitious way down to the harbour front, checking over his shoulder every now and then. By the light of a full moon, Fielding had no trouble picking out the Union Jack among the many ships in Callao Harbour. He limited his prospects to those lying at anchor at a distance from the docks—showing his face on a ship docked at the Callao wharves could be disastrous both for himself and for the captain who harboured him. Seizing upon a punt tied up at the nearest wharf, Fielding rowed out to the likeliest-looking of the lot, a handsome brig whose sides gleamed from a recent scrubbing.

"Ahoy there!" he hollered at the watch who observed him drawing closer. The man nodded noncommittally.

"You shipping out soon?"

"And who might be wanting to know?" the sailor asked, somewhat suspiciously.

"Me and my boy'd be needing passage back to England directly. Have you your full complement?"

"Sorry, mate," came the reply. "We've only just arrived and the captain's got business that'll keep us here three weeks and more."

"Obliged," grunted Fielding as he pushed away from the magnificent ship's side. He wondered if he should try a different tack and approach the next ship as a captain rather than as an ordinary seaman. It was a common belief among sailors that two captains onboard a ship spelled strife, but Fielding felt sure that he could act the part of a congenial companion to any ship's commander without calling into question the other man's abilities or authority. Fielding knew that he himself would never take another captain as a passenger on any ship he was commanding; now he would have to hope that other captains did not share his dislike for the practice.

He looked around for another ship, one less well-appointed than the first. A humbler ship might betoken a humble helmsman. He spotted a second brig whose best days seemed to be behind her. Approaching, he could see where oakum sprouted loosely from her seams and observed that her bowsprit had recently been replaced. Under the grime at her bow, he could just make out the name *Essex*. Pulling up alongside, he hailed the first man he saw on deck.

"Permission to board," he called out.

The watch spoke hastily to a second man who nodded, and the two of them lowered a rope ladder to Fielding.

"I'd like to speak to your captain," he said, once he'd made the ascent up the grimy sides of the brig to where the two sailors stood.

"He's gone ashore. I'll get you the mate," said the first man.

Fielding cordially introduced himself to the middle-aged balding man who shook his hand and proclaimed himself thrilled to make the acquaintance of a fellow Englishman, and a sea captain at that. The mate had spent time in Liverpool when he was a navy cadet and was interested to hear how the city had fared in the years since he had lived there.

"Just the same as you left her, I haven't a doubt," said Fielding. "A few more smokestacks and air not fit to breathe these past few years since the coke ovens came in full force. Shipyards bustling as always, only you don't see the slavers anymore. They're more worried about the fields these days than about finding men to work them—soil's mighty depleted from England to the Caribbean, and they're looking for better fertilizers to build it up again. That's how I ended up in Peru..." Fielding trailed off, suspensefully.

The mate bit.

"Tell me, sir, what brought you to these shores?"

Fielding smiled, emboldened by the mate's friendliness. "Some months ago I contracted with Myers and Company of Liverpool to ship a load of guano from the island of Chincha back to England. Either the company or the Peruvians must have blundered with the papers, because three weeks ago, I found myself arrested and my cargo confiscated. They impounded my ship and threw me in jail for theft."

"The Peruvians?" asked the mate in horror.

"The same," replied Fielding.

"But this is terrible! When our captain returns, I'll have him send advance word to the consulate in Valparaiso and have you reinstated."

"No need for that," said Fielding hastily. "I've already sent word, but my crew has meanwhile left for home on other ships while the mess gets sorted out. I'd just as soon wait it out, being out on bail, as you see, and free to wander the town at my leisure, but my son's picking up bad habits hanging around too many Spanish ports this past year. It's time for him to go to a good old-fashioned public school and get some learning."

The mate nodded. "I too have a son, just turned fourteen. Haven't seen him in three years, him nor my wife neither. We've had a rough time of it this voyage, but we'll be heading out soon—day after tomorrow if the weather holds."

Fielding adjusted himself in his chair. He hated asking for favours and was unaccustomed to it. "My predicament leads me to ask for passage back to England—me and the boy. The Peruvians confiscated whatever was left out of the wages after my arrest, so I couldn't pay for our passage. I'm sure that Myers would reimburse you for your trouble once we arrive in Liverpool." Fielding knew this was a lie, but was desperate enough for conveyance to say anything.

The mate shook Fielding's hand earnestly. "When the captain hears your story, I am sure that he and I will be of one mind—consider the ship your own."

Fielding stifled an insulting laugh at the thought of commanding a rotten hulk like this. The mate continued. "Come back tomorrow with the boy and there will be a berth waiting for you."

Fielding hesitated, dreading even one more night on the streets of Callao. "Might I trouble you for a place to sleep tonight?" he asked.

The mate looked surprised. "The captain returns in an hour or so. Come back then and he will speak with you."

After shaking hands with the mate, Fielding climbed back down the ladder and into the punt, and was soon gliding into the darkness. Crouched underneath the wharf a quarter-mile away, George waited anxiously for him.

Chapter Five

The voyage down to Valparaiso was the slowest imaginable, given the unfavorable winds and a leaking bow that kept most of the crew at the bilge pumps for the better part of a week. The captain of the *Essex* had been less charmed by Fielding than the mate had been and barely spoke to him throughout the voyage. Fielding guessed this had something to do with the old saying, "Two of a trade cannot agree." When they finally made Valparaiso, the captain was forced to face the inevitable: the *Essex* was not seaworthy and would have to be placed in dry-dock for major repairs.

The news hit Fielding hard. It would be nearly two months before a portion of the keel could be replaced and the vessel made ready for the high seas. Fielding was fed up. He decided to abandon the *Essex* and her taciturn captain in search of a faster way back to England.

His search soon proved fruitless. Few British ships at Valparaiso were homeward bound, and of those that were, none offered Fielding accommodation. The captains of the *Jeremiah* and the *Belfast* refused even to see him, giving Fielding the strong suspicion that news of the guano escapade had preceded him. Pacing disconsolately along the waterfront one day, he overheard a group of Spanish and Peruvian soldiers in conversation.

"So you say she's been condemned?"

"That's what Velazquez told me."

"What'll they do with the contents?"

"Auction them off to the highest bidder."

"And what's to become of *Vitula* afterwards?" Here Fielding felt the blood rush to his head in a dizzying flood.

"Unrigged and sold, they tell me. She's worth more in pieces than whole."

"How much is she worth, did they say?"

"At least ten thousand, maybe fifteen."

The other man whistled.

"More money than you and I will ever see, brother."

The sailors passed on their way.

Ruined. The word shrieked in Fielding's ear like a demon. At that moment, he knew he would never again command a ship, feel the thrill of authority over a large group of men who could be whipped for not obeying his orders. *Ruined.* It was the word that Fielding most dreaded—imagining the contempt with which other men would regard him, the shame that would haunt him until his death. He wiped the back of his hand across his sweating brow, hating himself for feeling afraid. So deeply sunk in despair was Fielding that he did not observe the handsome ship flying the British colours that was even now making its stately way into Valparaiso harbour.

The *Saladin*, a 243-tonne barque out of Newcastle and owned by Johnson and Cargill of that city, had been launched in March of 1835, under the command of Captain Alexander MacKenzie, master on this and all her voyages. Jutting menacingly out over her bow glowered *Saladin's* bronze-faced namesake, the famous Kurdish warrior, captor of Jerusalem at the Battle of Hattin in 1187, and adversary of the Christian king Richard I (Lionheart) of England. Richard's opinion of Saladin as a chivalrous opponent made the latter an icon among subsequent generations of English chroniclers of the crusades; for them, Saladin was the epitome of

Middle Eastern exoticism and mystique. Under a cream-coloured turban, Saladin's likeness knit his thick black eyebrows as though he had been insulted. His coal-coloured eyes glistened with seawater like tears.

As the ship prepared to drop anchor, Fielding turned his back to the ocean and made his slow way to Customs Square, at the heart of which stood his old friend La Nave, the only tavern he knew in Valparaiso where he was reasonably sure his pocket wouldn't get picked; he had but a few coins left, and he reckoned on spending them on liquor. His gold pocket watch, a gift from his father, had been pawned to pay for hotel expenses.

On board the *Saladin*, Captain MacKenzie barked out orders to his men.

"Look lively with those sails, laddies. I want 'em furled and stowed before I leave for town, and I'm a surly son-of-a-bitch when I haven't had me liquor. Faster you furl, faster you'll be rid of me for the night, and faster you'll be under the skirts of yonder Spanish lovelies. Ha!"

The men smiled grimly at the captain's joviality, a state they knew would not last long into the evening. Alexander MacKenzie was a mean drunk, and a frequent one, and the men aboard his ship were used to taking orders from the first mate, Bryerly, during the captain's periods of incapacitation.

"First watch'll take us to eleven o'clock. The next will come off at three tomorrow morning. You lads steer clear of any swarthy *senorita* offers you the Pisco brandy. She's like to put a shiv in your ribs quick as you'd look." MacKenzie winked at the mate. "Ain't it so, Bryerly?"

The first mate looked unfazed.

"Aye sir."

MacKenzie climbed down the ladder into the waiting longboat. "Adieu, laddies! Don't look for me ere morning light."

Fielding was well into his third glass of whiskey when MacKenzie entered La Nave, short of breath from a brisk uphill walk from the waterfront. Panting, MacKenzie called out to the barkeep in broken Spanish, "Pint of ale to start…keep it coming."

Fielding could detect the Scottish accent in its ill-fitting Spanish clothing and gazed quizzically though none too steadily at the owner of the brogue.

He saw a short man in late middle age, with thinning grey-red hair and mangy ginger whiskers that looked as though they'd been pasted on. This unpromising visage was dignified by a navy blue coat made of new broadcloth, upon which a straight line of gleaming brass buttons ran from throat to knee. *Ship's officer*, thought Fielding, *or else a regular sailor who cleans up well.*

He squinted to get a better look at the man's hands. They were clean and uncalloused—no rope-hauling in his recent past. Fielding revised his speculation: *Could be a captain.*

The barkeep, who had sprung to attention at the new arrival, seemed to confirm this theory by rushing out from behind the bar to shake the man's hand and to help him off with his coat, which he stroked appraisingly as he hung it up on a coat rack.

"*Bienvenido, Senor Capitan MacKenzie,*" he intoned gravely as the man took a seat at a table near Fielding. "You are special guest at La Nave. Anything you want. Anything."

"*Gracias,*" said MacKenzie obligingly. "That pint of ale'll do for a start."

As he put away the first of the evening's drinks, MacKenzie regarded the downcast Fielding. He knew he couldn't enjoy an evening of drinking in such melancholy company and decided that a new drinking companion would not go amiss.

"*Buenas noches, senor. Me…dar de beber a alguien?*"

"You'll think me a lover of Spaniards, but your butchery of their language is enough to drive a man to Compostela," said Fielding with a smile.

"Well, well, what have we here?" roared MacKenzie, happily surprised. "A bit far from home this evening, aren't we?"

"You took the words out of my mouth," replied Fielding. "What's a highland laddie like yourself doing in a place like this?"

"Many's the time I've asked myself that same question since we left Newcastle," MacKenzie spoke with feeling. "I've had nothing but troubles on this voyage. 'Twill be my last."

"Am I to understand that you are a captain?" asked Fielding.

"Aye," said the Scottish captain, moving over to Fielding's table. "Name of Sandy MacKenzie. *Saladin's* my ship; we got in just this evening. Brought her over fully loaded, but I hear trade's been slow this season."

"I can attest to that," said Fielding, bitterly.

"Are ye the master of some ship, or one of her men?"

"Master—until recently. My ship was confiscated by the Peruvians and her cargo sold at auction. I made it out of Callao with only the shirt on my back."

"What devilish business is this?" cried MacKenzie, genuinely shocked. "What cargo were ye carrying?"

"Guano, mostly."

"Did ye not have papers to show 'em?"

Fielding hardly hesitated. "Myers of Liverpool told me they had it settled with the Spaniards long before we hauled sails. Would I have come halfway around the world if I had doubted that?"

MacKenzie looked apologetic. "I'm sorry, lad. You must be sick about it. What's become of your crew?"

"Scattered to the four winds in Callao—they were a shiftless lot and I wish them ill, in the main."

"I dare say. I'm having difficulties with me own crew," began MacKenzie, glad to have a fellow sufferer at hand who knew well the nature of his woes. "It's been nothing but desertion of apprentices. They were a green lot when I took 'em on—never been to sea, didn't know the first thing about discipline. Ye well know how it is—weeks of incompetence and nothing but snivelling and sullen looks about their treatment. I wish 'em the navy, by God! Well, it was enough to drive a saint to violence—I had a few of 'em flogged, and it gave me profound satisfaction. Damn their hides! They begrudged and begrudged and took to their heels ere we made land at Buenos Aires for reprovisioning. Blast the lot of 'em, they've left me short a half dozen hands."

"They think they'll have an easier go of it on another ship?" Fielding asked incredulously.

"They'll not find a better ship than *Saladin*," said MacKenzie proudly. "I've sailed her eight years and never was there a finer." He drained the remains of his ale in a satisfied gulp and brought the glass down hard on the table. As if on cue, the barkeep issued forth smoothly with a second pint and quickly disappeared with the empty tumbler.

"Nice chap," MacKenzie nodded in the direction of the bar. "Been coming here for years, and the first round is always on the house. Have you tried the house specialty? Paolo!" he hollered in the direction of the barkeep, who had only just returned to his station where he was serving other patrons. He dropped his bottle and scurried to MacKenzie's side.

"Si, senor capitan? A su disposicion."

"Our friend would like to try the house special. Please add it to my account," said MacKenzie with a wink.

After Paolo had disappeared for the second time, Fielding asked, "What have you ordered?"

"A Chilean specialty, lad—Pisco brandy mixed with lemon juice, egg white and a wee skiff of powdered sugar—'tis beguiling."

"I don't usually go in for these queer foreign drinks; God knows what they put in 'em. But I guess brandy can't do much harm."

The waiter brought out the frothy amber-coloured drink, which Fielding swallowed in three gulps, just to have it over with. He barely tasted anything.

"There now, lad. 'Twas not as bad as all that, now, was it?" MacKenzie slapped him on the back, draining his own glass and calling immediately for another.

"I'd like to see her," said Fielding, turning his empty glass around and around in his hands.

"Eh?" said MacKenzie.

"*Saladin*. When do you sail again?"

MacKenzie reflected. "We're due for shipments of guano tomorrow and the next day, then some heavier stuff…" His voice trailed off, as the captain was suddenly aware of how freely he had been speaking to a stranger. In truth, the *Saladin* would be carrying back to England seventy tonnes of copper, thirteen 150-pound bars of silver (both mined in Chile), a large quantity of expensive spices, and a ship's chest full of dollars and money letters. MacKenzie knew it wasn't wise to itemize his ship's full bill of lading in front of anyone, not even his crew, the majority of whom he intrinsically distrusted.

Fielding noticed MacKenzie's hesitation and was immediately on the alert. What kind of additional cargo did the captain not want him to know about?

MacKenzie regained his composure.

"Come around tomorrow morning and I'll show you the ship. She'll warm the cockles of your heart, she will. Come around ten." MacKenzie reckoned that tomorrow would be a safe time for visiting, before the arrival of the precious metals from the country's interior later in the week.

"I'll do that," said Fielding decisively, standing up and holding out his hand.

MacKenzie stood and shook it warmly. Fielding turned to leave.

"Wait!" called MacKenzie suddenly. "You haven't told me your name, lad!"

"Haven't I? George Fielding."

"Your servant, Captain Fielding." MacKenzie bowed to the younger man, then straightened and raised his glass in a toast.

"Your servant, Captain MacKenzie." Fielding tipped his hat to the Scottish captain and quickly made his exit.

Chapter Six

By his fourth day of wandering the hilly slopes of the port city, George had come to the conclusion that of the towns and cities he had seen on this long voyage, Valparaiso was his favourite. Perhaps it was simply the familiarity bred by a second acquaintance with the city that warmed his heart, but there were other things too. The morning sun rising over the Andes to the east made each day dramatic; the way the city seemed to cling to the hillside before sloping sharply into the Pacific seemed a wondrous thing. He was getting used to hearing several languages spoken among the men who crowded the waterfront warehouses, and had no trouble finding English speakers there. It was an English sailor on shore leave who told him the reason why Valparaiso, or Valpo, as he called it, had no real docks—fearing an attack from its northern neighbour, Peru, the Chilean government had had only one floating wharf built twenty years earlier; this could be hauled up in case of a Peruvian attack. Of course, that was before the big earthquake and the tsunamis swept everything away.

At the city markets, George lingered over the delightful fruits and vegetables of the Chilean south: Indian corn and beans were staples at every market stall, complemented by ripe peaches, bunches of red and white grapes, and a strange, plump, green fruit that George had never seen before. Seeing his puzzled stares, a kindly merchant offered him one—biting into its succulent flesh, George thought he had never tasted anything so delicious as this ripe fig.

When he could tear himself away from the fresh fruit tables, George often spent a few pennies on other Chilean foodstuffs: the dried beef called *charqui* that would keep for days in a boy's pocket, delicious-smelling corn *tamales*, which vendors kept hot over coal or wood braziers, and *empanadas*, baked dough rolls that sometimes contained chopped beef, sometimes chicken, and sometimes cheese. George loved them all.

Most mornings, George would buy his breakfast at the market with money he had pocketed among the waterfront drunks of the night before. Eating a *tamale* or a piece of *charqui*, he would walk back to Customs Square to look for his father, whom he knew would likely be skulking around La Nave. George usually arrived hot and out of breath, for it was an uphill walk; he wondered how the Spanish ladies in their heavy black dresses and long veils always seemed to arrive at church cool and collected on similar walks. George usually found his father slumped over his stool in the tavern or trying to engage sailors in conversation in the hope of finding passage home to England. George still worried about getting home, but found Valpo so much to his liking that an extended stay there did not upset him. The weather was so balmy, with the sea breezes always keeping the humidity in check—maybe living here wouldn't be so bad.

On the fifth morning, George did not find his father at La Nave, nor anywhere else in Customs Square, where the international traders congregated. Puzzled, George decided to walk back down to the waterfront to look for him. As he walked, a terrifying thought took hold of his mind and would not let go: *What if he's left without me?* George shrank from the possibility of being left behind in a strange land. Almost as soon as the thought had come, new thoughts crowded in. *I hope he has gone without me. I am better off without him.* With a start, George realized that he had been pretty well looking after himself these past few weeks, with his father gone most of the time. George had even been giving his father money for drinks at the tavern while they had been in Valparaiso. He had been doing just fine without Fielding's help—better than with it, now that he came to think of it. A new world began to open like a flower unfolding its petals before him. He might do as he pleased with no one around to criticize and belittle him, as his father had done, or to irritate him with demands that he go to school, as his mother once had. *What good did school ever do anyone,* George reflected. He might get hired on as a hand on one of the English ships that docked at Valparaiso and continue his sea adventure without his father. What a relief it would be not to have to hide whenever he heard Fielding's voice!

He had reached the waterfront and was caught up in its bustle, elated by his newfound freedom. As he passed a ship loading large crates of guano, he felt a firm hand on his shoulder.

"There you are, you alley cat—were you trying to run away? I've had the devil's own time looking for you. You'll stay close these next few hours; I've got work to do and don't want you running off."

George's heart sank as his father's hand propelled him into a crowd of sailors leaving one of the taverns. It was clear his father had another scheme in mind. George felt a heavy cell door clank shut within his soul, trapping him forever.

Within the hour, Fielding had engaged in conversation with several of the English-speaking sailors George had seen exiting the tavern. Four of them joined Fielding and his son as they made their way back to the makeshift floating wharf upon which the bulk of the *Saladin's* cargo was sitting, about to be loaded. One of the men walked with a peculiar limp.

On the deck of the ship, George could see a flurry of activity as hands worked to stow the guano below deck. Surveying their work was a small, ginger-whiskered man in a blue coat. Fielding hailed him from the wharf.

"Hullo! Captain MacKenzie, sir!"

Turning, MacKenzie recognized Fielding and waved. "You're early, Cap'n Fielding. We're still taking on cargo, as you can see. But welcome, all the same." As he spoke, MacKenzie slowly descended the gangplank towards them. His head pounded painfully, the fruit of his last evening's labours at La Nave.

"Good morning, sir," Fielding greeted him warmly. "This young man here is my son George. Shake hands with the captain now, boy." He pushed George forward.

MacKenzie weakly grasped his hand. "Pleased to meet you, laddie." Then, to Fielding, "And who are these other gentlemen? I thought you'd be coming alone this morning."

"These men are looking for employment aboard *Saladin* in whatever capacity you see fit. This one here goes by the name of George Jones." Here Fielding indicated the man with the limp. "Says he'll work his passage over and can make sails. An Irishman, he tells me."

MacKenzie looked surprised.

"Well, now. And where did you find these men?"

"Met 'em this morning coming home from the taverns. I heard you mention last evening that you were short a few men so I thought I'd help you round up a crew. These fellows got friends that would swell your numbers to what's required."

MacKenzie was quiet for a moment. He stammered when he spoke.

"That's a mighty decent thing you've done, Fielding. You've saved me a heap of trouble, lad."

Fielding smiled. "Of course, you'll want to look 'em over for yourself, make sure they're up to the task. They gave me a fair account of themselves coming over from the taverns, though—I think I can vouch for most of them."

MacKenzie's eye rested somewhat dubiously on George Jones, who, it was now obvious, wore a wooden leg.

"How'd you lose that leg, lad?" he asked, none too solicitously.

"Fell off a spar when I's young, sir," replied Jones in a husky, County Clare accent.

"Get around alright on that stump, do you?"

"Yessir."

"Show me," demanded the skeptical captain.

Jones paced a large circle around MacKenzie, concluding this performance with a few jig steps. He was used to having to account for his disability with ships' masters.

MacKenzie looked nonplussed. "And you can mend a sail?"

"Yes sir. Done it my whole life."

"Who'd you last ship with?"

"Captain Goreham, *Heart's Delight* out of Liverpool."

"You quit her crew?"

"Sir, with due respects to that captain, it was an unruly crew that fought like cats all the way to Valparaiso."

"So you'll take your chances with *Saladin?*"

"Sir, my desire is to return to Ireland and my poor mother before she dies—I'll render my services without pay should you give me passage."

"Commendable, commendable," nodded MacKenzie. "You shall have it. If you've no other kit," he gestured toward the small chest at Jones' feet, "you may join the others. The mate will enter you on the muster roll. Bryerly! Ho! Bryerly! Come out here!" MacKenzie shouted up at the deck of the *Saladin.* A head soon emerged from beneath the deck of the ship.

"Yes, sir?"

"My friend here has supplied us with a crew; I'm sending the first of the lot up to you. Show him the quarters and enter him on the rolls."

"Very good, sir. I have the ledger in my hand." The first mate looked relieved at the sight of Jones and the other men standing on the wharf.

"Go on, then." MacKenzie gestured impatiently at Jones. "Look lively with that stump."

"Thank you, sir." Tipping his hat to MacKenzie and Fielding, Jones picked up his chest and hopped up the gangplank. On deck, clearly in his element, he blended instantly with the rest of the toiling hands.

"Well done, Fielding!" MacKenzie slapped his friend on the back heartily. "If the rest come out as well as the cripple, we'll be ready to ship in no time. What else do you have for me?"

Fielding introduced John Galloway, a nineteen-year-old Scottish youth, the son of a bookseller and a member of a prominent family in Stranraer. Galloway told MacKenzie that he'd left his last ship when wages weren't paid, but that he'd been learning navigation and had attained a modest competency. MacKenzie regarded him with interest; the lad had a cunning look about him—his dark eyes took in everything and revealed nothing. *Too smart*, thought MacKenzie for a moment, then dismissed the thought as foolish. *You may need his navigating ere long; one never knows what can happen on a long voyage.* He shook hands with Galloway to seal their agreement and sent him up the gangway after Jones to be mustered.

The other men proved to be satisfactory, and one by one, they too joined the *Saladin*'s crew after a brief dockside interview with their future captain. Soon, only MacKenzie, Fielding and George remained on the wharf.

"Well, dear lad, you've been a godsend, and that's the truth of the matter."

"'Twas nothing—I'm sure you'd have done the same for a fellow captain," replied Fielding, looking at MacKenzie somewhat expectantly.

MacKenzie started. "But—I had almost forgotten—will you and your son not join me for tea in my cabin? 'Twould be especially remiss of me not to invite you aboard after the kindness you have shown today. Gentlemen?"

"We would be delighted," smiled Fielding, nudging George in the ribs.

"Delighted," echoed the boy uneasily. He knew his father was up to something, and suspected what it was. Fielding's generous and friendly behaviour this morning was too far out of character to be trusted.

MacKenzie revelled in showing the Fieldings every corner of his ship, from stem to stern. Fielding exclaimed over each detail in a way that made George even more uneasy.

"Must be grand to be in command of so fine a vessel," he remarked, as they sat in MacKenzie's cabin, sipping tea from English bone china that made George homesick for Liverpool.

"'Tis indeed, friend."

"If I only had a way of redeeming *Vitula*, how happy I would be!" Fielding lamented in a voice too loud to be affecting.

"'Tis a blight on all Peru what they did to you and to your ship," MacKenzie sympathized. "Dirty Spanish scoundrels! What outrages will they not hesitate to perform upon the hapless seaman who tries to make a living in international waters?"

Fielding latched upon this last sentence. "Indeed, sir. Their actions seem more grievous when viewed in that light. The island where we removed the guano must be twenty miles off the coast—I doubt whether it is even a Peruvian possession."

"An act of piracy, sir, plain and simple. You said you were carrying English goods at the time of the seizure?"

"Yes—worth a small fortune," said Fielding, warming to the subject and to being the aggrieved party.

"No doubt they were just looking for an honest seaman such as yourself so as to seize upon his goods and his ship. Unscrupulous bastards, the Spaniards. No doubt they make a practice of this sort of thing, if truth be told."

Even Fielding found this scenario laughable; it was highly unlikely that the Peruvian navy would engage in high-seas piracy against a country whose empire encompassed one quarter of the world's population and whose superior navy was fully capable of blockading the coastline or reducing the Peruvian navy to a smouldering ruin.

Still, for the sake of the scheme he was at pains to carry off successfully, he continued with the game. "No doubt it is as you say, my dear MacKenzie."

There was a pause as MacKenzie reached inside his coat and pulled out a silver flask, adding a healthy dose of its contents to his teacup. He sipped delicately.

"Yes indeed…Now. Fielding, may I ask what your immediate plans are?"

Fielding hesitated for a moment. "My object is, of course, to return to England at the earliest possible opportunity. George here has been away from school too long, and I have a sick wife waiting in Liverpool. I dare not tell her of the disaster that has befallen us in Peru; she would die of the shock of it."

MacKenzie looked genuinely sympathetic, while George stared at his father in disbelief at the brazenness with which he had spoken this untruth.

"You are beset on all sides, dear man," MacKenzie said softly, offering Fielding his flask.

Politely declining, Fielding rose as if to leave. "My dear MacKenzie, we have troubled you long enough, and I must commence again my search for passage for my son and me." He laid a fatherly hand on George's shoulder that made the boy's flesh crawl.

Before he knew what he was doing, MacKenzie had leapt to his feet and called for the mate. "Bryerly! Come here instantly!" he yelled. The harried Bryerly soon appeared at the cabin door.

"Enter Captain Fielding and son as guests of *Saladin* on the roll. No arguments, Fielding," he held up a warning finger as Fielding made to protest this generosity. "I can't very well leave you to the tender mercies of the Peruvian courts after the help you've been to me," he said warmly.

Fielding was jubilant, but attempted to look humble. "If I had a cent to my name, you should have it for your kindness to me and my little son. As it is, we shall ever be in your debt." He bowed low to the captain.

"Get up, get up," said MacKenzie, gruffly. "I am certain that Messrs. Myers will have the papers well in order when we drop anchor in Liverpool. We can settle accounts then."

Fielding smiled ruefully.

"We await only the last shipment of minerals from the interior before setting sail." MacKenzie was still reluctant to divulge the specific contents of the shipment. "I'll have Bryerly show you your quarters." He added, "It'll be a blessed relief to have someone to talk to other than numbskulls and pedants on the return voyage."

Fielding laughed heartily. George continued to stare at his father, shocked at his gall.

Bryerly, too, looked somewhat taken aback by the sudden increase in personnel aboard the *Saladin*.

"Bryerly!" MacKenzie's bark jolted the mate. "Where is your ledger, man?"

"I'll see to it, sir. I was in the middle of mustering the new men when you called, sir."

Bowing to Fielding, Bryerly hastily exited the cabin.

"Good man, that, but a nervous disposition. The slightest noise sends him into fits," remarked MacKenzie as he poured more whiskey from his flask into his teacup, stirring it demurely with a teaspoon.

At that moment, a deep growl was heard from the captain's bunk, and the blankets atop the bed began to shift and twitch as though alive. George was terrified; his father, badly disconcerted.

"Go back to sleep, Toby," called the captain amiably to the growling lump. "You're having a bad dream. All is well, dear boy."

After another anguished twitch, the lump on the bed gave a deep sigh and was still.

MacKenzie grinned at the discomfiture of his guests. "'Tis merely my dog, Toby, gentlemen. A fine English bulldog bought in Newcastle. Meek as a lamb, but a watchful guard at night."

Fielding nodded sagely. It was as he had thought: MacKenzie must have a valuable cargo aboard. "A gun's as good as a dog any day, but a man can only fire one when he's awake," he reflected.

"Well, laddies," said MacKenzie, standing up suddenly. "I must get back to me work. Go and find Bryerly; he'll see to all your necessaries. Dinner's at seven—come back to the cabin then and I'll have the cook lay in a nice meal. Good day!"

MacKenzie climbed, none too steadily, up the ladder to the deck, leaving Fielding, George, and the sleeping Toby alone in the cabin.

"Well, boy," said Fielding with a broad grin. "We'll live to see jolly old England yet, though they may still hang us when we arrive."

George frowned at being included in this dismal fate, but said nothing.

"The world ain't through with me, by God, not by a long shot," said Fielding in a quiet voice, as though speaking to himself.

George knew that his father was in earnest and feared for the world.

Chapter Seven

The captain's new guest arrangements were the cause of much below-deck grumbling well before the ship's departure, as Bryerly informed Jem Allen, who served as the ship's carpenter, that two new berths were to be added to the officers' quarters for the Fieldings.

"Close enough quarters without two more added in," remarked Allen, as he dragged extra lumber into the tiny cabin where he, Bryerly, and Galloway already slept.

"Indeed," replied Bryerly ruefully, hauling the current occupants' trunks out of the way to make room for the new bunks. "I don't know where MacKenzie expects us to keep our things. Perhaps I shall remove to one of the longboats to sleep."

The two men laughed at this, but Bryerly was only half-joking. He was a light sleeper and hated the sound of snoring. A quiet rest at the bottom of a longboat would be the answer.

The mysterious mineral cargo destined for the *Saladin* arrived two days earlier than expected—an unusual circumstance—and with the winds favourable, MacKenzie decided to weigh anchor the morning after the loading was completed.

It was a crew of ten, plus the captain and his two passengers, that sailed from Valparaiso that morning in early February, 1844, aboard the heavily laden *Saladin*. MacKenzie anticipated a rather difficult fifty-day voyage to Cape Horn battling the southeast tradewinds, then a refit at Montevideo before tackling the trans-Atlantic portion of the journey home.

With the first light of day and with a brisk breeze blowing to seaward, MacKenzie ordered all hands on deck and began the laborious process of setting the sails and weighing anchor. He waited at the helm in readiness to take the wheel while the first mate, Bryerly, supervised the raising of the sails and the second mate Moffat directed the raising of the anchor and the untying of the line from the mooring buoy. George Jones and two others now put their backs into the windlass, and small groans and whistles escaped their lips as the sweat appeared on their foreheads. William Johnston, one of Fielding's new recruits, had lowered himself into a rowboat alongside the mooring buoy behind the stern, and was now unsuccessfully attempting to untie the rope; the knot securing the rope to a ring on the buoy proved to be hopelessly tangled, and Johnston cursed it thoroughly.

With nothing now securing her to the harbour bottom, the *Saladin* began to move, her bow swinging toward shore like a pendulum, still attached at her stern to the buoy, which Johnston now frantically tried to untie. With the stern tied, MacKenzie had no control; he frantically fought the wheel, trying to bring the bow back into the wind, while he watched with horror as the ship's prow struck the end of the nearby makeshift pier with a sickening crash.

"Haul off! Haul off!" yelled the captain to the distracted crew, who for the moment were oblivious to the fact that they were still partially moored and believed that MacKenzie had ground the ship into the pier in a drunken miscalculation. Only Carr, the cook, who had been standing at the ship's stern, saw the source of the problem. Snatching an axe from the heap of tools dropped by Allen when the ship had collided with the pier, he began to chop frantically at the taut rope still tethering the *Saladin*. The rope was thick and put up a strong resistance to his efforts. From the rowboat below, he could hear Johnston cursing at the other end of the rope and wondered which end might give first. With a sudden crack, the rope snapped apart, lashing the air like a burned snake. The *Saladin* began to drift away from the pier in response to MacKenzie's tug on the wheel. Bryerly now called for the jib sheets to be rapidly hauled in; the *Saladin* swung away from the pier and into the wind.

"Trim the mainsails, men!" ordered Bryerly, and the ship quickly gained forward momentum.

With MacKenzie still at the helm, Bryerly and Allen darted forward and down into the ship's hold to check for structural damage. Five minutes later, they returned topside and gave MacKenzie the good news: the hull planking at the bow showed no signs of being displaced and there appeared to be no leakage. MacKenzie said nothing, but stared straight ahead while the mates addressed him. Further inspection confirmed that the worst injury the *Saladin* had received in the incident was an ugly paint scrape on the starboard side of the bow above the waterline.

It was fifteen minutes or more before anyone noticed Johnston's absence. He was back near the shore, waving frantically to get the crew's attention. Bryerly ordered the sails loosened, and the *Saladin* floated with flapping sheets while several men lowered the longboat and rowed back to collect the stranded and irate Johnston.

The longboat back in place, Bryerly had the jib sheets hauled in and the main sheets retrimmed. The *Saladin* was finally on her way.

But for the cook's presence of mind, the ship might have been badly damaged, and MacKenzie now indiscriminately vented his pent-up fury on the hapless crew. Bryerly was the closest to the captain and so received his opening volley.

"What in God's name did you think you were doing, man?" he demanded in a belligerent tone. "I suppose you realize you could've wrecked the ship back there."

"I, sir?" said Bryerly, twitching slightly with surprise.

"You, sir." The usually flushed colour in MacKenzie's cheeks had deepened to a hectic scarlet and his voice quavered with rage.

"Begging your pardon, captain, but 'twas yourself at the wheel at the time of the collision. I was engaged in setting the sails as ordered."

"Well, then, who is responsible?" barked MacKenzie.

"No one, sir," ventured Bryerly. "Each man was doing his job: Jones was hauling the anchor and Johnston was in the boat, untying us from the buoy. 'Twas an accident, plain and simple."

"And where was Allen while all this was happening?"

"Waiting to give the signal to Jones and Carr to ship anchor when I had the sails up and ready."

Spotting the offending officer just over Bryerly's shoulder, the captain stormed past the mate and confronted the unsuspecting Allen. "There you are, you sorry bastard. Explain yourself! Give me one reason why I shouldn't have you flogged for dereliction of duty."

The soft-spoken carpenter studied MacKenzie's flushed face and said nothing for a moment. He was a decent man and a good navigator, without question MacKenzie's equal in seamanship. He could have held a position of ship's master himself but for his reluctance to shoulder the responsibility of the job. He knew that the pressures of being the helmsman on a trade mission could often make a captain's temper snap, and so did not respond in kind to MacKenzie's insult; he did not wish to breed enmity between them at the commencement of a long voyage.

"I assume you refer to the accident at the pier, sir," he began.

"What else?" snapped MacKenzie.

"In that case, sir, I can tell you that I was standing amidships near Bryerly, who was directing the sails. Johnston couldn't see me down at the buoy so I had Carr stand at the stern to pass on my signal to untie as soon as I gave it. When Bryerly had all the sails up and was ready to set them, I gave Jones and Carr the signal. Johnston couldn't get the line untied, and that's when the accident happened. It was no one's fault."

"And you did nothing to help cut the line or come to Johnston's aid in the boat?"

"What could I have done, sir? By the time I could have cut through the line or climbed down to Johnston, we were already free."

"The words of a pedant who'd sooner die than do a tap more work than absolutely necessary. Get out of my sight," MacKenzie waved Allen off with a gesture of disgust. Allen was only too glad to leave him.

Seeing Jones limping about on deck attending to his tasks, and with his blood still up, MacKenzie cornered him against the starboard railing.

"I want a word with you, you Irish bastard."

Jones' suspicious blue eyes glowered beneath a shaggy fringe of dark hair and heavy black eyebrows; never one to take blame when not warranted, he bristled now at the captain's insult. "I'd imagine you're out lookin' for a scapegoat for a foul-up clearly of your own making. Are ye the captain of this ship? Why was it the cook and not the captain that got us out of this scrape?" he sneered at MacKenzie.

The captain drew a sharp breath, then slapped Jones hard across the face. "Insolent dog!" he roared, losing sight altogether of the original intent of the dressing-down. "I knew the minute I laid eyes on you that you'd be trouble—poxy Irish always are—and a damn cripple into the bargain. I'd horsewhip you right here and now, but for I can't spare any hands on this ship even for the time it would take to rig it for a flogging. As it is, you'd best stay out of my sight 'til we reach Liverpool, or by God, I'll take that wooden stump of yours and beat you with it 'til you're dead!" And off he stormed.

Laughing derisively, Jones made a deep bow to the retreating captain's back and grabbed his groin in a gesture of defiance. Johnston saw it—had, in fact, been listening to the whole of the heated exchange from where he stood swabbing the foredeck. He beckoned to Jones.

"Collared, was you, Jones?"

Jones shrugged. "Bastard's just out looking for someone to blame, but no one fingers George Jones with impunity."

"You sure got him worked up," Johnston smiled, clearly impressed with Jones' performance. "He won't be fit to live with for days, I reckon."

"He'll cool off," said Jones, lighting the pipe he kept tucked into a breast pocket.

"But he's made an enemy today."

As the *Saladin* continued on its slow exit from Valparaiso harbour, George, who had been below decks at the time of the accident and had missed its bitter aftermath, emerged from the officers' cabin and walked slowly along the deck, staring wistfully into the ship's wake and at the city he had grown to love, which he knew in his heart he would not see again. Already Valparaiso's tall Roman Catholic church spires were growing more diminutive by the minute, and the hillsides behind the city seemed shrouded in an otherworldly mist. George felt tears prickling his eyes and a lump growing painfully in his throat. How he hated his father at this moment! In one decisive gesture, he had pulled the boy away from his mother and friends in Liverpool, and now he was pulling him away from a city George wished he could call home. The boy wept silently while the soft offshore breeze dried the tears on his cheeks.

As the ship entered the open waters of the Pacific, an uneasy silence prevailed on the *Saladin*. Allen and Bryerly, accustomed to MacKenzie's angry outbursts, had long since allowed the incident to slide off their backs. The same could not be said of Jones, who harboured an injured pride and a festering hatred for MacKenzie that trickled down to his new friend, Johnston, with whom he shared instances of MacKenzie's incompetence, both real and imagined.

Though they never would have dared speak openly about it, several of the crew thought MacKenzie was a fool for taking on another captain as passenger. At the very least, Fielding's presence would be a distracting influence upon MacKenzie, whose propensity for drinking needed little encouragement from a convivial companion to be transformed into a raging binge. Bryerly was already quite used to taking over command of the *Saladin* when the captain was incapacitated by drink and its painful aftermath. The mate was of the opinion that two captains aboard a ship spelled trouble and did not trust Fielding. Rumours were rife about Fielding's escape from a Callao prison, and few on the *Saladin* doubted that he had, indeed, been guilty of theft at the time he was apprehended. Further acquaintance with Fielding did not endear him to the carpenter, who only grudgingly spoke to the passenger, nor to the cook, who, though pleasant enough in his address, always seized upon the earliest opportunity to escape from conversation with Fielding.

Sensing that he was something of a *persona non grata* on board the ship, and finding his waking hours increasingly long now that he wasn't in command, Fielding redoubled his efforts to befriend the men. Overhearing Jones' daily litany of complaints about MacKenzie to Johnston as they sat mending a torn sail one day, Fielding deftly inserted himself into the conversation.

"Pardon me, lads, but I couldn't help but overhear—am I to understand that you have cause for dissatisfaction with our good captain?"

The two men clammed up, regarding Fielding with suspicion.

"An' if we did, would we be likely to tell you about it— the captain's cherished guest of honour?"

Fielding laughed. "You say that as if we're bosom friends—hardly, lads, hardly. I'm just passing the time of day with men I helped find employment. Of course, if you don't feel like talking, I'll be happy to take myself elsewhere…" Fielding's voice trailed off, as though hurt by the men's rejection. Seeing this, Jones repented somewhat of his impoliteness toward a superior who had done him a favour.

"Pardon me, sir. We meant no disrespect. We were just bellyaching about how the captain never takes the blame for anything that goes wrong on this ship. Take the bump at the pier in Valpo: he blamed everyone but himself and it's been more of the same since. Just like a Scot—stingy with everything, including giving credit where it's due. You should've heard the curses when Bill here dropped a bucket of dirty water on deck yesterday. You might've thought he'd betrayed us to the Spaniards, the way MacKenzie let loose on him. He's every bit as cussed as that damn mongrel he keeps under wraps in the cabin—both of 'em sons of bitches would tear your leg off quick as you'd look!" Johnston nodded vigorously in agreement with his friend.

Fielding put on an appropriately aggrieved expression as Jones spoke, though he had no quarrel with MacKenzie's tactics; the two captains shared the belief that most sailors were lazy dogs given to fits of self pity that had to be whipped out of them in order to make a productive crew. Fielding saw at once that Jones was the sort of man who held grudges, always looking for opportunities for revenge—a man he both despised and identified with.

Seeing Jones' pipe was empty, Fielding proffered his own tobacco pouch.

"'Tis a shame to see dissent in the ranks, lads," he intoned piously, "though, now that you mention it, I have noticed that you two have received more than your share of his wrath these past few days. I shall speak to the captain about it over dinner tonight, if you think that might improve relations."

Johnston, ever quick to seize upon an opportunity, jumped to his feet. "Bless you, Cap'n Fielding. Any good word you could put in on our behalf..." his voice trailed off.

Jones kept his seat, eyeing Fielding coldly. "An' if you could see your way clear to getting a hold of some of the captain's grog when he's well in his cups, we'd be mighty obliged, sir." Jones could, of course, have found a way to gain access to the captain's liquor cabinet, but if someone were going to get caught pilfering, he'd rather it be Fielding.

Fielding tipped his hat to the two men. If MacKenzie's liquor was the way to the sailors' confidence, why, it would be like taking candy from a baby. In the dinners of the two preceding nights in the captain's quarters, MacKenzie had begun pouring rum before the plates were cleared away and had continued imbibing well into the night. On both occasions, he had fallen asleep in the middle of the same story about surviving the great African typhoon of 1839, and Fielding had crept back to the officers' cabin unnoticed.

No matter how drunk MacKenzie became, Fielding could not get him to talk about the mysterious cargo the *Saladin* was carrying, nor would the captain even let Fielding near the manifest itemizing its contents. Fielding suspected it was kept under the mattress where Toby dozed fitfully most of the day, occasionally emitting deep-throated snarls and growls when the ship lurched suddenly or when a loud noise disturbed his slumber. Fielding did not care to test the good nature of the beast whom many of the crew secretly called "Antichrist."

The evening after his conversation with Jones and Johnston, Fielding and MacKenzie were sitting at dinner in the captain's cabin, having just polished off a rather salty meal of corned beef, cabbage, and potatoes. Above them, through the cabin's large skylight, the diners could see the stars of the southern hemisphere beaming brightly.

"Carr tells me he had the devil's own time getting a hold of them tatties in Valpo," said MacKenzie with a smile as he poured the first round of rum. "Seems corn and beans are all of what's available at the markets this time of year, but things have been improving with the British navy presence on the coast. You see far more good old-fashioned wheat biscuits nowadays, where before it was all cornmeal."

Fielding nodded absently.

"I see you and Jones in conversation a fair amount these days," said MacKenzie in a casual tone. He paused expectantly, but Fielding didn't take the bait.

"There's a snake in the grass if ever I saw one," continued MacKenzie. "We weren't even clear of Valpo Harbour before he gave me some lip about hitting the pier—all my fault, don't you know, not the mate, not Allen, not that dog Johnston, and especially not George Jones!" MacKenzie ended sarcastically. It was clear that the incident still rankled with him and that he expected a sympathetic audience in Fielding, a fellow captain.

"Who was it had the docking of the ship when you first arrived? Bryerly?"

"I'm the captain; I docked her," said MacKenzie querulously.

"You pulled her in awfully tight to the wharf."

MacKenzie bristled.

"Of course I did—we were loading crates of guano. I wanted to get as close in as I could to make the job go faster."

Fielding nodded. "That's likely what drove her into the wharf. I've seen the like many times."

MacKenzie's temper flared. "Just what do you mean by accepting passage on another man's ship and then telling him how to run it?"

"I've done no such thing. But a captain should take responsibility for his ship—and be able to admit when he's made a mistake."

"The only mistake I made was giving you passage on *Saladin*. I've never met such an ingrate!"

Fielding rose from the table.

"I think I'll retire for the evening. Good evening, sir."

"Good evening, my arse. I'll thank you to keep your opinions to yourself in future—and stay away from Jones while you're at it. By God, I don't trust either one of you."

Fielding turned and left the captain's quarters, his fists clenched in his pockets.

The next day, a chilling silence permeated the ship's atmosphere as the two captains sedulously avoided each other—no easy thing in such limited quarters. Fielding made a point of conspicuously conversing with Jones whenever the latter came off watch and sought him out in the men's quarters with the flask of rum he had surreptitiously filled at MacKenzie's table the night before. Fielding had taken subsequent meals with the officers, and MacKenzie dined alone.

Taking a long swig from the flask, Jones eyed Fielding with interest. "So. You and the captain ain't on the best of terms, it seems."

"It would seem not," said Fielding, non-committally. "He hasn't said a word to me since I suggested that he might have been at fault when we collided with the wharf."

Jones laughed. "I imagine he hasn't! Old bastard can't admit when he's been wrong."

"We find ourselves in the same proverbial boat, Mr. Jones."

Jones whistled. "Some boat. This here's a treasure ship, cap'n."

Fielding's ears pricked up. "A successful trading venture was it, then?"

Jones nodded, rummaging his pockets for his pipe. "Aye, sir—I kept my eyes open when MacKenzie was checking the lading bill back in Valpo—we're a floating bank, cap'n."

"Recall any of the particulars?"

"Indeed I do. Seventy tonnes of copper, a tonne of silver, nine thousand in spices, and a chest full of dollars and money letters."

Now Fielding whistled. His stomach seethed with jealousy at MacKenzie's trading successes as evidenced in the rich cargoes he now carried. "Not bad for an old man! That's a hell of a lot of chinaware to palm off on the Spaniards."

"MacKenzie always gets his price, the men say," said Jones.

Fielding felt another surge of jealousy. "Too bad he's too drunk most days to take the wheel," he said derisively. Jones laughed. "Maybe some day he'll fall overboard in one of his fits."

"Aye, sir—we'll throw the dog after him and be done with the pair of 'em."

"What then, Jones?"

"Why, you'd have to take the helm, cap'n," Jones said only half-jokingly.

Fielding looked at Jones a moment. "I suppose I would, if it came to that."

Their conversation was interrupted as two crewmen came off their watch and shuffled into the cabin. Twenty-eight-year-old John Hazelton wore a mean expression on his dark and whiskered face and a malingering stoop in his shoulders. The younger and more personable Charles Anderson, a native of Uddewala, Sweden, was chattering away in broken English to Hazelton, who looked as though he'd had enough conversation for one evening. Fielding had recruited both men for MacKenzie just days earlier, and he greeted them warmly now.

"Evening, gents," he said. "What word from above decks?"

Anderson smiled. "The sky clear, we have seen Southern Cross tonight."

Hazelton scowled, none too pleased at seeing Fielding in the crew's quarters. "Beg your pardon, sir," he said sharply, "but that's my bunk you're sittin' on at present."

Fielding stood up, apologizing.

"Well, you boys get your sleep. I'll leave the flask with you—sorry it couldn't hold more." Turning to Jones, he said in a quieter voice, "We'll continue our conversation tomorrow." Jones nodded.

Throwing himself down, fully clothed, on his now-vacated bunk, Hazelton questioned Jones.

"What the devil are you doing, talking to Fielding?"

Jones shrugged. "Any of your concern, John?"

"I don't like him down here—captain gets wind of it, and he'll be on us like a chicken on a dough dish. I don't want that and neither do you, George."

With surprising swiftness, Jones crossed the floor and seized Hazelton by the collar with both hands.

"Listen here, mate. George Jones speaks with whoever he pleases, whenever it suits him. Do you mark me?"

Hazelton nodded, momentarily stunned.

"Good man." Jones smiled, releasing the collar and backing away from Hazelton's bunk. "I felt sure you would understand my position."

"You're a strange bastard, Jones," said Hazelton, too exhausted for the moment to continue the dispute. "You'll get us all killed before this journey's over, you and Fielding." Rolling himself tightly into his overcoat, he fell asleep immediately.

Returning to his own bunk, Jones pulled out a bottle containing linseed oil and turpentine, and with an old handkerchief, began polishing his wooden leg. A pleasantly astringent smell filled the cabin.

Meanwhile, Anderson picked up the piece of whittling he had begun the previous evening and began slicing pieces off it with his pocketknife, an old ritual that he believed helped him sleep through the night.

Seeing the concentration Anderson applied to his task, Jones called cheerfully over to him. "You Swede—try to whittle at my leg while I'm asleep and I'll cut your throat."

"Ya, Jones," laughed Anderson uneasily. Though taller and possessed of a more athletic build, Anderson was clearly afraid of Jones, whose wooden leg he regarded with superstitious fear.

With little to occupy his time, Fielding filled his days in conversation with whatever crew members would talk to him and making mental observations of the way MacKenzie ran his ship. He couldn't resist the occasional jab of criticism that he knew would have the captain foaming at the mouth.

"You're beating awfully sharp against the wind, you know," he began one day, as MacKenzie stood on the quarterdeck. "You'll have your sails in tatters before we reach the Horn."

MacKenzie gripped the *Saladin*'s rail with a force that could have splintered it.

"Since when did you become the captain of this ship?" he asked through clenched teeth.

"Slack her off a bit and we won't lose significant speed. You'll be doing your rigging a hell of a favour," replied Fielding.

MacKenzie exploded. "I rue the day I ever laid eyes on you at that damn rathole La Nave! You've been nothing but trouble since Valpo, you meddling bastard. I pull you from the jaws of the Peruvian army, and what thanks do I get? It's clear to me now—you're nothing but a liar and a thief, and I'll be the first to tell the authorities the moment we drop anchor. I wish now I'd left you to rot among the Spaniards, but I'll settle for seeing you hanged when we reach Liverpool."

Fielding walked away a few feet, leaned against a bulkhead and stared coldly at MacKenzie. As the captain turned his back to Fielding, Jones, who had witnessed the altercation, saw Fielding make a slicing gesture across his throat and mouth the words "Damn you."

Jones felt an unfamiliar chill come over his body as though the temperature had suddenly dropped. He shivered as he watched Fielding walk briskly away. Seized by a fear that he didn't fully understand, Jones crossed the deck to where MacKenzie stood and grasped the captain by the arm.

"Please sir," he began earnestly. "I have to speak with you—Captain Fielding—he... just now... he threatened..."

MacKenzie brushed Jones aside with a gesture of disgust. "You damned Irishman. I want to hear nothing."

Jones retreated as quickly as he had approached.

Chapter Eight

The idea that had sprouted in Fielding's mind just after leaving Valparaiso had been fed and nourished well by its progenitor's greed in the weeks that followed. It took firm root and grew strong in the hatred that surrounded it, and gradually choked out all other ideas. Fielding knew that mutiny was a serious business; the faintest whiff of it was enough to see a whole crew put in irons, and when he was a captain, it was his greatest fear next to fire. But he was a captain no longer. At night, as he lay in his bunk listening to the wind catching the sails and the steady slap of the waves against the *Saladin*'s sides, he fell prey to the anxieties that had sprung up in his Peruvian prison cell: the horrors of ruin and the poverty and social stigma it entailed, being an object of scorn and, worse, of pity. Of course, he wouldn't have to worry about these things if MacKenzie carried out his threat of testifying against him on reaching Liverpool; if he were tried for theft and evading lawful authorities, Fielding knew he could face life imprisonment, even hanging. These were the thoughts that churned like a whirlpool in his mind, scouring out any fragments of hope that might have still remained.

It was usually after several painful hours of sleeplessness that Fielding allowed the idea of mutiny to take hold—it offered a strange comfort to his troubled mind. At first, he entertained visions that precluded actual murder: an early fantasy of Fielding's involved a convenient attack of ship's fever that carried away all but a few members of the crew and himself, allowing him to take command of the ship and its cargo. Who could call such a tragedy mutiny?

Inevitably, Fielding's mind turned to darker scenarios—like a short and brutal dispute with MacKenzie that left the captain knocked unconscious while Fielding and his carefully selected henchmen slit the throats of the two mates and dumped all three men overboard.

Sometimes, even in the midst of these fantasies, Fielding could not tell whether he was driven by greed, desperation, or hatred of MacKenzie—or a combination of the three.

As the *Saladin* approached the continent's nadir, Fielding knew with a growing certainty that he would carry out his idea. The morality of it was something he chose not to think about, for the thinking would surely drive him mad. He trusted in a forgiving God, as much as he could recall from his sporadic church attendance, and let the rest go.

Fielding needed accomplices, that much was certain. With the ship entering the most dangerous phase of her homeward journey, there was little time to speak with the crew, all of whom were engaged in the minutiae of keeping the *Saladin* afloat. MacKenzie lashed them on with still greater ferocity as the weather worsened and the mercury sank in the glass. The winds howled and the waves rose high above them like white-flecked mountains, as with tightly reefed sails they rode the crests and dropped with sickening force into the hollows, over and over again.

"Damn the eastward drift—this is the worse we've had of it since leaving Newcastle!" yelled MacKenzie to Bryerly as the two men stood amidst the pitch and dip of their craft as she reeled under the strain of the storm. It was too dark to see the coal-coloured smudge of Cape Horn to the north, its icy crags beckoning sailors to their doom.

By great good luck, however, the weather passed and the *Saladin* crossed uneventfully from the Pacific to the Atlantic, to the immense relief of the captain and crew. Now that they had passed the Horn, MacKenzie put Jones to work at mending sails. Jones was just as glad to be out from under the captain's thumb in the cabin, where he had witnessed MacKenzie's excessive drinking. It was hard for Jones to maintain respect for a man he had to carry away from the table unconscious and put to bed almost every night.

As his drinking increased, so did MacKenzie's irascibility. Anderson discovered this one morning, when he had taken over the helm for Allen while the latter finished some on-deck repairs. The carpenter had cautioned him that he was a little off-course.

"Bring her back a little, Charlie."

In attempting to correct the ship's course, Anderson over-swung by a couple of points. MacKenzie had been nearby during this exchange and arrived at the helm just as Anderson overcorrected.

"What the hell's the matter with you? Can't you hold a steady course? Let me see you right us," he slurred, exhaling a strong reek of whiskey.

Flustered by the reprimand, Anderson now swung the wheel too far in the other direction.

Without another word, MacKenzie hauled off and drove his fist hard into Anderson's right shoulder, knocking him off balance. He hit the deck with a dull thud, humiliated more than injured.

"Allen! Take over from this worthless cretin." The captain walked away, cursing under his breath.

The carpenter helped Anderson to his feet. The Swede's eyes were burning with rage.

"Have you ever hated a man enough to want to kill him?"

The question took Jones off guard. He and Fielding were sitting together on a coil of rope, mending sails. Fielding had just threaded his needle and was about to pierce the torn canvas with it. Jones stared at him for a moment. "Why you ask, cap'n?"

"Suppose there were a mutiny. Would you strike a blow against the captain?"

Jones hesitated in his stitching. "I never killed anyone and I don't care to start now, sir."

Fielding regarded him with coolness. "You may not have a choice, Jones."

The other man looked shocked indeed. "What in heaven's name are you about?"

"There's trouble aboard. MacKenzie has enemies among the crew. If you want to save your life, you'll say nothing and do what I tell you. You'll make up your mind now, or lose your life."

"You intend to be master of *Saladin*, then?"

"Aye. I can tell you no more at present; it would do you no good to know."

Jones said nothing, too stunned to speak.

Fielding stood up. Placing his index finger near his lips, he made a quiet shushing noise. "Mark you—talk, and you forfeit your life. I speak with Johnston tonight."

Paralyzed by dread, Jones felt as though he had been turned to granite where he sat. He felt the chill of death upon him.

One by one, as the days wore on, Fielding approached other members of the *Saladin*'s crew and swore them into his deadly compact. Johnston was the easiest: Fielding knew he would do whatever Jones did and that he nursed his own grievances against MacKenzie. Hazelton was harder; for days, Fielding observed his behavior, waiting and watching for an opportune moment to spring his trap. When the moment came one night below deck, it was the promise of a share in the *Saladin*'s riches that turned the tide in Fielding's favor and won him Hazelton's loyalty. *Every man has his price*, Fielding reflected as he left the cabin, a look of grim determination twisting his mouth into a grimace.

Fielding did not approach Bryerly or Allen with his plan, nor Moffat, nor Collins. All had regarded him with varying degrees of suspicion at one time or another on the voyage, and would remain loyal to MacKenzie 'til death, Fielding was sure. He knew that Carr was an honest man and would want no part in murder; he would have to be done away with accordingly. Galloway was far too scholarly and correct to join in the mutiny but could be easily subdued, if necessary. But would four men be enough to overcome seven? The odds bothered Fielding. He had not yet spoken with Anderson.

He found the Swede alone in the galley peeling potatoes late one afternoon and made his approach.

"There is going to be curious work on board," he said.

"What is that?" replied Anderson.

"Jones, Hazelton, and Johnston are going to take the ship and kill MacKenzie. I will be in command."

Fielding's words had an unexpected and immediate effect.

Gripping the knife he held in his right hand, Anderson spoke in perfect English, as though he had been silently rehearsing the words for days:

"By God, I'll take this knife and cut his throat. He shall no more strike me away from the helm."

Fielding looked puzzled. He was not present when MacKenzie had dealt Anderson the blow that sealed his fate.

"You will join us, then?"

Anderson grabbed Fielding's hand and pumped it up and down in a fit of compulsive handshaking. His laughter was high-pitched and maniacal.

Wednesday, the tenth of April, about three hundred miles south of the equator, Carr succumbed to the cold sweats he had felt coming on for days and took to his bed. Bryerly entered him in the sick column of the ledger, where he remained for the next three days. George, too, had felt unwell for some days, and he was more than happy to keep to his cabin, out of the sight of his father and the men who seemed to distrust him.

Carr's absence from the galley made it an ideal haven for the conspirators. The men—Jones, Johnston, Hazelton and Anderson—sat huddled around the coal fire at half-past ten on April thirteenth, summoned there by Fielding, whose haggard expression and frenzied, darting eyes told of his many nights without sleep. His words to them were brief and direct: "Tonight we take the ship—Bryerly is the first, then MacKenzie, Allen, and the men forward. You will follow my orders. Any man who denies my orders will be killed. It must be done tonight."

Listening as though to his death sentence, Jones felt the dread he now associated only with Fielding, whom Jones had come to believe had cast a spell upon him and the other men. A hundred times since Fielding's threat, Jones had tried to bring himself to approach MacKenzie and apprise him of the wickedness simmering in the breast of his hated passenger, and a hundred times, cold fear held him back. He now felt himself a traitor to both captains and despised himself for his cowardice. Crazed with fear, he prayed over and over, "Blessed Mary, mother of God, have mercy on my wicked soul for what I am about to do."

With Allen asleep until the morning watch of four o'clock, Fielding now sent the men to collect the tools the carpenter kept carefully stowed beneath a tarpaulin beneath the longboat: axes, hammers, and mauls that had been instrumental in keeping the ship afloat these long weeks would now be used to cut down their owner and his mates.

It would be Jones, Hazelton, and Anderson under Bryerly on the middle watch, midnight to four o'clock. The killings would be done between those hours.

The men sat in the galley and waited. Anderson whittled on a piece of firewood until it was a pile of sawdust on the floor. Hazelton read parts of the Old Testament aloud in a toneless voice: "If I whet my glittering sword, and mine hand take hold on judgment; I will render vengeance to mine enemies and will reward them that hate me."

Jones listened to the sound of his breath as though in a trance.

A stirring from the officers' quarters, and Bryerly appeared on deck, looking flushed in the light of the ship's lantern. He, too, was sick with a fever. Concealing their weapons as best they could beneath their oilskins, the conspirators joined him at the helm while Fielding hid in the shadows.

Leaning against the wheel, Bryerly spoke to Hazelton in a faint voice,

"Jack, steer the ship as well as you can. I don't feel very well."

"Aye, sir. Why don't ye take a rest?"

"I may do just that," said Bryerly, grateful to be relieved of his duties.

The hencoop was just a few paces away, and Bryerly laid down on top of it, pulling his oilskin around him to stop the shivering that periodically convulsed him. He closed his eyes, oblivious to the noiseless approach of Fielding and Johnston from the shadows.

Fielding leaned over the mate's sleeping form and gestured to Johnston, who swung the carpenter's axe in a deadly arc, smashing Bryerly's skull. All the air left Brylery's body in an "oh" sound, and his blood poured like a summer downpour off the roof of the hen coop. Inside, the chickens, startled in their sleep, cackled briefly then were silent. Dropping the axe, Johnston hoisted the body by the shoulders with Anderson at its feet. Swung overboard like a heavy sack, the body dropped into the sea.

At the helm, Hazelton reeled and choked back vomit. He had no weapon. It was Fielding, Johnston, and Jones with axes, Jones with a knife as well, Anderson with a claw hammer. An axe waited for Hazelton. Now the men stood above the captain's cabin and stared in through the skylight at the sleeping MacKenzie.

"You will kill him in his sleep," said Fielding flatly.

They had not touched the cabin door before loud growling from within backed them away. Toby!

Fielding waited for them on deck. "So it is done?"

"The dog, sir! The whole ship'd be up in arms with his barking and us with our throats torn out before the deed was even attempted."

The captain's bell rang sharply twice, and Jones felt a sharp stab of fear between his ribs: MacKenzie was clearly awake, roused by Toby's growls. The bell was likely the summons for Galloway and the whiskey bottle. The mutineers held their breath, frozen to the spot. Would the bell wake the remaining men? Ten slow seconds passed. Could the ambush of the sleeping sailors proceed?

Hazelton ventured a whisper to his mates: "Moffat's a sound sleeper; Collins too, I'll wager. The others, I don't know about."

As he spoke, Allen, a light sleeper, rose from his berth in confusion. The bell was a voice calling him in half-sleep.

"Who calls me?" he sang out, his throat thick and uncleared.

Still on the ladder, the carpenter was seized by the throat and dragged the rest of the way up. Johnston held his mouth shut; Anderson swung the claw hammer, but did not kill him. Allen screamed as he fell over the side, yelling "murder" from the waves where his white head bobbed eerily in their wake like a buoy.

Now, all was confusion. Hearing Allen's cries from the water, and forgetting Fielding's deadly pact, Jones cried out again and again in concert with his sailor's first instinct, "Man overboard!"

Heeding the same instinct, the captain yelled from below, "Put the helm hard down—back the main topsail!" For a moment, it was as though good will still prevailed on board the *Saladin*.

Rushing up the companionway, MacKenzie was met squarely by the blunt end of Anderson's broad axe. "You will never again strike me away from the helm," the Swede gasped at the captain even as the latter, unhurt, wrenched the axe out of his grip. "You ruffian—I will take your life!" exclaimed MacKenzie.

Infuriated, Fielding grabbed Jones and shoved him towards the pair who struggled for control of Anderson's weapon.

"Lay hold of him or I will give you a clout that will kill you!"

Jones felt the noose tighten around his neck; he stepped between the combatants, and began prising MacKenzie's fingers loose from the axe, Anderson bending out of the way of the jerking blade. *A strange dance*, Hazelton thought afterwards, as three men clasped each other in brutal intimacy.

"Strike him!" yelled Anderson to Fielding, whose own axe hung poised above his head like an executioner's. Anderson and Jones waltzed MacKenzie closer to the murderer's blade.

MacKenzie jerked sideways, and Fielding's axe skidded wide of the mark, slicing into his victim's left shoulder. MacKenzie sank to his knees, whispering curiously, "Oh, Captain Fielding! Don't."

Fielding's next blow parted MacKenzie's skull neatly. Jones and Anderson slipped twice on fresh blood before sending the corpse overboard.

Fielding dropped his axe.

"Gentlemen, the ship is ours! Let us drink to this great occasion."

Trembling and blood-soaked, the men followed Fielding to the captain's cabin. Toby, shut in when MacKenzie had quit the cabin moments earlier, now lunged for Fielding's throat. In that moment, a flash of metal passed between the two, and the dog seemed suddenly to be caught short; he whimpered as he slid to the ground, Fielding's knife buried in his chest.

"I've wanted to do that since we left Valparaiso," said Hazelton, kicking the corpse as he passed by.

Fielding filled MacKenzie's washbasin for each man to scrub his hands clean of blood before they drank. Spying the captain's Bible resting on the washstand, Fielding eagerly seized it, saying, "It is well that we should each swear an oath of allegiance to one another on this holy book: May *Saladin's* spoils be divided equally among all five of us, just as the five of us have shared in the killing of our enemies."

Anderson was the first to take the oath, his right hand planted firmly on the cover. He was followed by Johnston and Hazelton. Fielding swore next. Jones would not touch the Bible—it seemed to him to glow with an infernal heat that he knew would scorch his palm when wielded by the devilish Fielding. Johnston and Hazelton had to hold him down while Fielding held the book to his hand, and Anderson, a knife to his throat, before he would swear.

"Now I am damned," he whispered, as they released their grip on him.

The men quickly passed around the first bottle of the captain's best twelve-year-old scotch whiskey, brought from Nairn and jealously hoarded for a special occasion. The liquor's effects took only some of the edge off the memory of their still-fresh brutality. Over the next two hours, they finished off another bottle, silently gathering their courage until four o'clock, when they heard the stirring of the men of the morning watch, Moffat and Collins, below deck.

Hazelton and Johnston slipped back to the positions the new watch would expect to find them in, while Jones and Anderson concealed themselves beneath an old tarpaulin once used to cover firewood. Though they were not yet done with killing, the magnitude of the crimes they had already committed was beginning to dawn on them. All were heartily sick of bloodshed. It was MacKenzie they took issue with, not the men who served under him, but Moffat and Collins would never agree to mutiny—and so their fate was sealed.

"Morning, Jack, Bill," said Collins sleepily. "Give me a moment while I attend to urgent business." He unbuttoned his trousers and stood at the rail, sending a stream of urine cascading into the ocean.

It pained the cheerful Anderson to end a man thus exposed, but an oath was an oath. The deadly claw hammer connected with Collins' skull, sending his bleeding, unconscious body toppling headlong over the rail.

Moffat had just emerged from the men's quarters and saw the hammer still in Anderson's hand. "What's this, Charlie?" he exclaimed. Johnston and Hazelton replied with twin blows to the head with their axes. Moffat's lifeless body soon joined the others in the night-black ocean.

Fielding and his four henchmen stood on the foredeck of the *Saladin,* her decks running thick with blood. It was just after four o'clock and the sun had not yet shown itself on the horizon. Fielding's eyes gleamed in the lantern light.

"Now the ship is ours," he murmured, more to himself than to his men.

Below decks, Carr, Galloway, and George slept on, oblivious to the carnage that had taken place.

Chapter Nine

In the oppressive atmosphere created by the murders, there still hung the question of what to do with the cook and the apprentice navigator, still asleep below decks. Fielding had been hesitant to execute Galloway because of the fine navigational skills he already possessed, which might prove useful at a later stage of the voyage. He was still unsure about Carr. Delirious with fever for three days and nights, the cook had not shown himself on deck or in the galley since well before the murders, but he was showing signs of recovery and would soon need to be considered. Fielding hated the idea of further dividing the *Saladin*'s spoils in exchange for Carr's silence when they reached port, and so resolved that the cook should not live.

On Sunday, the fourteenth of April, Carr woke near dawn, feeling better than he had for a fortnight. He rose from his sickbed and put on a clean shirt, then started for the galley to light the fires for breakfast.

Glancing toward the starboard side of the ship, Carr thought he was still in the grips of delirium; the whole deck appeared to be tinted a deep red. Carr rubbed his eyes and shook his head—no, it was still red, and sticky to the touch.

"What in the name of the good Lord has happened?" he asked aloud to no one in particular.

"Stay where you are, Bill," said a voice from the poop deck.

Carr looked up and saw Fielding flanked by Johnston and Anderson, both armed with pistols stolen from the captain's cabin. Hazelton stood nearby.

"What is the cause of the blood spilled on the deck?" he demanded, advancing.

"I said stay where you are," snarled Fielding. His men raised their weapons.

"You heard 'im, Bill," said Johnston.

"I am in command of this vessel now," Fielding continued. "Hazelton is first mate and Johnston is second mate. The master and crew have gone away and left us."

Carr glanced around the ship—longboat and gigs were all intact.

"It can't be," he said, confusedly. "All the boats are here."

"That's right," Fielding said, smiling. "We have finished them—MacKenzie, Bryerly, and the men. The Lord have mercy on their souls." Hazelton crossed himself with the tip of his pistol.

At the men's feet lay what Carr now realized with horror were the instruments of his fellows' deaths: the carpenter's axes and hammer, and Carr's own hatchet. He shuddered at its appearance among the heap of murder weapons.

"This is a serious circumstance." Carr spoke as though he were in a nightmare. Could he still be suffering from the fever? When would it break? The cook broke down in tears.

"Indeed it is," answered Fielding. "Will you join us?"

Carr sobbed, "I would rather go overboard with the rest."

Hazelton called out, "We don't want that, now, Bill. We've had enough bloodshed around here. Besides, no one among us makes better grub than you."

Anderson laughed loudly, a shocking sound at the scene of so many deaths.

"If I do not join you," said Carr, when his sobs had subsided somewhat, "I suppose I must go the same road as the others."

Fielding looked conciliatory. "Now, Bill, you see that the deed is done and we are all to share equally in *Saladin*'s spoils. In return, we ask merely for your silence. It is plausible that the men died of ship's fever, is it not?" He winked at the cook, whose terror temporarily disabled his speech. Carr could only nod his assent.

Fielding smiled. "Good man, Bill. You are of our counsel then, and can help the men with the disposal of weapons. There'll be no more killings on this ship. Weapons breed mutinies." The new captain uttered these words with not a hint of irony.

Anderson and Johnston looked at each other for a moment, then gathered up the carpenter's axe and claw hammer and threw them overboard. Carr picked up a knife and his own hatchet and sent them to their fate.

"What about the captain's rifle?" asked Hazelton. "He keeps it in his cabinet—I'll fetch it."

"No," said Fielding, quickly. "It may prove useful in shooting fowl on the voyage."

The men looked at each other again.

"Now," said Fielding, "Someone must acquaint Galloway with the night's doings—Johnston! Wake him and bring him to me."

The young navigator was brought on deck in a daze and stood before Fielding. He was rumpled from sleep and looked frightened as the captain told him of the murders.

"Well, John," said Fielding. "Are you of a mind to join us?"

Galloway quickly snapped out of his fog. "I am, Captain Fielding. Indeed, I should have liked to have had a licking at the old man before you sent him overboard."

Johnston snickered.

Fielding regarded the lad with an appraising look. The conspirators had never made overtures to Galloway to be a part of their plot, assuming by his quiet, scholarly demeanor and eagerness to please those in authority that he was a MacKenzie loyalist. Still, there was something about Galloway that suggested the canniness of a politician with an eye on the main prize. Fielding distrusted him.

"Well, then, lad. You are our principal navigator. Go below to the captain's cabin and spread out the charts. I will be with you in a trice."

Galloway quickly vanished below deck, followed by Carr. Turning to his henchmen, Fielding said, "They shall both die before the voyage ends. For the moment, though, we are in need of their services. Five men cannot easily man a ship of *Saladin's* size—with those two alive, there will be less work for each of you." The men nodded in assent.

Later that day, Fielding set about the work of re-establishing order on the ship. He ordered a course north by northeast and the ship was put about. The men were divided into two watches: Johnston, Carr, and Galloway in one, and Jones, Anderson and Hazelton in the other. Gathering the seven men together in the evening, Fielding put forth his plan for their immediate future. They would sail the *Saladin* to Newfoundland, unload the ship, and hide everything of value on the island. Then, the crew would travel to the Boston states and charter a schooner, returning some time later for the *Saladin's* hidden cargo.

Johnston spoke up. "Sir, why don't we throw the copper overboard? It's slowing us down considerable—what if we are apprehended before reaching the North Atlantic?"

Fielding scowled at him.

"What, and throw away our most valuable cargo? That copper's worth as much as the silver and all the money on board! No—we'll take our chances at an open sea between here and Newfoundland. Now, boys, shall we have a look at what the old man was keeping to himself all these long weeks?"

The men entered MacKenzie's cabin and began breaking open the sealed chests containing letters destined for faraway families and friends in England. Any money found inside was removed and the letters burned. The men rampaged through MacKenzie's quarters, smashing open the captain's desk, chests of drawers, and trunks in search of money—all under Fielding's orders. MacKenzie's personal effects were divided up with glee. The men were unused to well-made clothing and a dispute soon broke out over a pair of the captain's trousers. Fielding settled it by seizing the trousers himself.

Johnston had charge of the watch coinciding with the dividing of the spoils. He felt resentful and uneasy, both at not being present for the pillaging, and at being on a watch that included the doomed men, Carr and Galloway. He was fast growing suspicious of Fielding's motives, and feared for his own safety. Over and over he asked himself, *Why am I put with Carr and Galloway? Is my life worth more than a ship's cook?* He knew it would be an easy matter for Fielding and the other watch to take his own watch by surprise. He suspected it would be done in the dead of night, as with the other murders. The thought preoccupied him constantly. He finally determined to share his fears with Carr early one morning when the second watch still lay sleeping below deck.

"You know, Fielding has sworn to kill you and Galloway before we ever make land."

Carr blanched and said nothing.

"If they try to murder you, I will die fighting to save you." Johnston spoke in earnest, and Carr was moved by the sincerity he saw written on the sailor's face. The cook was momentarily struck by how young Johnston looked, his features softened in the lamplight. It was a face that Carr would long be haunted by.

"You can count on me likewise, Bill, should the need arise. Them devils'll not get the better of us." The two men shook hands warmly.

Galloway was in MacKenzie's cabin after the ransacking had ended, trying to restore some degree of order to the chaos that now prevailed. He wished to use the captain's quarters for a study and had set up a table and chair in the corner brightest from the light coming through the skylight, where he could spread out his charts. It was here that Fielding found him three days after the murders.

"You're a bright young man, John," Fielding's speech was smooth, rehearsed.

"Thank you, sir."

"How far did you get in your studies before you shipped out?"

"Not as far as I'd've liked, sir."

"What are your plans for the future?"

Galloway looked at Fielding cautiously. He knew that no question from the captain was innocent. "Don't know yet, sir. University, perhaps."

Fielding smiled. "You'd be needing funding for that enterprise, John."

Galloway said nothing, rolling a pencil back and forth between sweating palms.

"*Saladin* could be your patron. Think about how much more of its riches could be yours were there fewer men to share it with."

"How many fewer?" asked Galloway suspiciously.

"Johnston, Jones, and the cook—that's three. That would leave us with enough men to sail her to Newfoundland."

Galloway put down his pencil. It rolled from one side of MacKenzie's desk to the other with the movement of the waves.

"Captain Fielding, sir. I cannot take part in what you propose. I would die first."

Fielding frowned, surprised by the young man's adamance.

"Suit yourself, then." Turning, he left the young navigator to his charts.

Fielding next approached Anderson as he sat whittling on his bunk that evening.

"I was just talking with young Galloway about a way of increasing our profits on this enterprise."

"How?" Anderson asked.

"By ridding ourselves of Carr, Johnston, and Jones. We don't need them to run the ship. You can cook as good as Bill and that Jones has been nothing but a curse since before we got rid of MacKenzie, with his moping and staring. Johnston is superfluous—Hazelton is the better seaman. That would leave us with a crew of four, with my son as a fifth." It was the first time Fielding had thought of George in days.

Anderson regarded Fielding evenly.

"Serious matter, captain," he said slowly. "Let me think. We talk tomorrow." He returned to his whittling. Fielding nodded, not discouraged with Anderson's cautious approach. He was a slow-witted fellow that the captain figured would come around to his way of thinking eventually.

But Fielding had misjudged Anderson. The frightened Swede sought out Hazelton and Jones as soon as the captain left the cabin and told them of Fielding's murderous plot. Jones' hands shook as Anderson spoke. His delirium of fear had not abated since the killing of MacKenzie and his men and he had barely slept. A dark figure seemed to hold a knife to his throat every night as he was about to drift off to sleep, waking the terrified Jones with a start. He regretted with all his being that he had ever participated in so evil a business as the murders on the *Saladin*. He now profoundly wished he could join the everlasting rest enjoyed by MacKenzie and his men. He knew that for himself there would be no rest again.

The diminished crew of the *Saladin* felt a dread keener than that which had possessed them before the massacre. Then, they had been motivated by opposing feelings of comradeship and self-defense—feelings stirred in them by Fielding, who had assured them that their fellows had already agreed to be part of the mutiny and that those who did not participate were in mortal danger. The promise of a share in the ship's wealth had stirred them to a murderous fever pitch. Now, with MacKenzie disposed of and the *Saladin*'s riches spread out before them, none of the men seemed able to glory in the overthrow, to contemplate a life of ease after the ship had been disposed of and her crew dispersed. Instead, they felt a renewed fear for their lives that centred around Fielding, the man who had conceived the mutiny. The plan he now was setting before them—the taking of more lives for no reason other than financial gain—seemed gratuitous and brutal. They had had enough of bloodshed and knew, though they did not speak of it, that their lives had been forfeited with the first stroke of the axe against the mate.

Chapter Ten

It was Johnston who found the two pistols in Fielding's cabin. The captain, who had been drinking heavily since the murders, had fallen out of his bunk and was making a terrible racket. Johnston had heard his curses and had reluctantly come to his aid. It was then that he had seen the pistols on a table near Fielding's bed, partially covered in a canvas wrap. Seizing them swiftly, Johnston turned on the inebriated Fielding.

"What's this, then, captain? Two pistols? We made an agreement to throw all our ship's weapons overboard, didn't we?"

Fielding looked cornered.

"Damned if I know where those came from…could have been the old man's. Tell Anderson and them to search the ship. Who knows what else is aboard…"

Still holding the pistols, Johnston left the cabin and went immediately to the galley where Carr was stirring a pot filled with ham shanks and split peas.

"Look what I found on the captain's bedside table, would you, Bill?" Johnston dumped the pistols on the table with a clatter.

Carr's mouth gaped open. "Well, I'll be damned. So he planned on doing his own killings this time. Have you shown the others?"

"No, I haven't. I wanted you to be the first. You'll agree that something needs to be done about Fielding, I hope?"

Carr nodded vigorously. "Go and find Jones—I'll look for the rest on deck."

Johnston looked grim. "So many murders and Fielding wants more killings. Something must be done."

Carr looked impatient. "Yes, Bill, yes. Let's find the men."

Anderson reacted violently to Johnston's discovery of the weapons. He began pacing the deck and rubbing his hands together, muttering "He cannot live. He must not live," in a low voice.

Jones, meanwhile, proposed that the crew carry out an extensive search of the *Saladin* for more weapons, with any findings to be disposed of immediately. The men agreed. With Carr at the wheel, the crew set about their task, soon uncovering a copper canister filled with gunpowder in one of the captain's lockers. Breaking open the spirit-locker, a large carving knife was found, along with two bottles of brandy. Johnston opened one and dipped a finger into the liquid, then passed it along his tongue. He quickly spat out the residue. "Poisoned," he grunted to Hazelton. "Go ask Carr if he's been missing a knife from the galley."

"Indeed I have," came the shouted reply from above deck a few moments later. "Has that devil Fielding taken it, indeed?"

The men, armed with the pistols, gunpowder, and poisoned liquor, now converged on Fielding's quarters, where the captain, still the worse for drink, was lying on his bunk, his hand covering his eyes.

"We wish to have a word with you, sir," Johnston began, still holding the two pistols.

"What is it?" asked Fielding in a querulous voice, not uncovering his eyes.

"We made an oath, sir," said Johnston, "an oath at which we were all present. We swore to be as brothers and to throw all weapons overboard as a token of good faith. Do ye recall this oath, sir?"

"Of course," said Fielding, uncovering his eyes and taking in the group of men who stood before him.

"Why then, sir, did you feel it necessary to keep two pistols in addition to the old man's fowling piece and Carr's carving knife?"

Fielding looked blankly at Johnston and at the pistols he carried. "Where did you find those?" he demanded.

"They were left out in broad daylight for any fool to see—here in your cabin."

"They are mine—give them to me." The drunken Fielding made an unwise lunge towards Johnston, who stepped to one side; Fielding sprawled to the floor.

"Tie his hands, boys," ordered Johnston, and Fielding's hands were quickly bound behind his back by Anderson and Hazelton.

"You have broken your oath, Captain Fielding, and have made death threats against members of the crew. You have poisoned the men's drink. You are a danger to the safety of the ship and her men. We shall keep you restrained in this fashion until we have decided what is to be done with you," said Johnston.

Fielding set up a hue and cry, peppering the air with curses. Johnston ordered that he be gagged. "We've heard enough from you, Captain."

Working the gag out of his mouth with great difficulty, Fielding spluttered, "I'll not have you treat me like a slave. Take me on deck—I will throw myself overboard. There is nothing left for me now. Throw me overboard!"

"Shut him up!" growled Johnston, and Anderson stuffed the gag back in Fielding's mouth. "Charlie!" Johnston continued to Anderson, "You take the first watch over him. The rest of us will confer on deck."

"What'll we do with the bastard?" said Jones to Johnston once the men had left Fielding's quarters. "I'm damned if I'll take another life after the other night."

Anderson spoke next. "Galloway and Carr...they can push him overboard. They kill no one yet."

Johnston nodded, warming to the idea. "The Swede speaks true. Why should we be the only ones with blood on our hands?"

Galloway shook his head emphatically. "I won't do it."

"It's like this, lad," said Johnston. "Either you are with us or you're with Fielding. Will it be him over the side or you?"

Galloway was adamant. "It'll have to be me, then. I'll not bloody my hands."

Hazelton interjected. "Why can't we keep Fielding and the boy confined in the forecastle and put them off in Newfoundland? Then none of us'll have his killing on our conscience."

Jones shook his head grimly. "As long as he's alive, he'll see to it that we all hang for what we did."

Hazelton and Johnston nodded in agreement.

"I'll not sleep until I see that bastard safely over the side," said Carr with uncharacteristic ferocity in his voice.

"Then you must both do your part," said Johnston to Carr and Galloway. "Come, it must be done."

The men returned to Fielding's cabin, where the captain's attempts at escape had reached a frenzied pitch. His wrists and ankles were chafed raw and bloody against the roughness of the hemp that bound them. His eyes were bright and rolling with terror.

"Stand him upright," Johnston ordered Carr and Galloway. The latter crossed his arms and refused to touch Fielding.

"Do it!" yelled Johnston, grabbing Galloway, but the apprentice sagged in his grasp, making a dead weight of himself as he had often done when the village bullies had attacked him as a small child. Johnston dropped him with disgust.

"Damned coward," he spat at Galloway, turning his attention back to the prisoner. "Jones, help haul the bastard to the deck."

Dragging the bound and struggling captain to the deck proved almost more than two men could handle. The gag slipped again as they reached the deck.

"You sons of whores! You'll never do it! I'll live to see you all hanged from a sour apple tree! Damn you all to hell…"

"Galloway, grab a hold of his feet!" ordered Johnston.

"No!"

His father's screaming roused George from his sickbed, where he had lain, unattended, for three days, with only a jug of water at his bedside. He had had no appetite for food. It was a terrifying sight that greeted him now as he dragged his weakened body up the rungs of the ladder to the deck. Carr and Jones had Fielding balanced precariously on the railing, his hands and feet bound securely like a bundle of firewood. They held him steady while Johnston and Anderson gripped the terrified Galloway between them, yelling, "Touch him! Touch him, you yellow bastard!"

George cried out, half-delirious, "Are you murdering my father?"

Ignoring the boy's cry, they waltzed Galloway closer to the bound victim, now in his final death struggle like a fish gasping in the deadly air.

Anderson got hold of Galloway's right arm, and propelled it forcefully toward the railing.

"A little push is all it takes—see?"

Galloway's hand toppled Fielding off the rail and into the dark ocean below.

George let out a howl and rushed towards Carr and Jones, kicking, biting, beating them with his fists.

"Now the boy," said Hazelton. "We'll have no acts of revenge. Too bad you was the son of such a son-of-a-bitch." He spoke with something like sympathy in his voice.

"Galloway!" yelled Carr, pinning George's arms behind his back. "Grab his feet!"

Galloway moved as though in a nightmare, compelled not by his own will, but by a dark force that seemed to take possession of his mind and body and overmaster them. He grabbed the weeping boy's ankles. There was little struggle left in him.

"Please—please," cried George. "What have I done? How have I deserved to die?"

There was no answer from the crew of the *Saladin*.

Galloway swung the boy's legs over the edge, but George maintained a tight grip on Carr's jacket.

"Let go, now," said the cook sternly, as though disciplining a child. "Let's get this over and done with."

"Please, sir, please…" There was a sound of tearing fabric as the cook tried to shake himself free of his burden. The material gave up like a sail torn through by the wind and the child plunged into the waves with a scream.

Carr turned back to face the men with tears on his face.

"It is a terrible thing to see a child die," he said in a voice too quiet to be heard before retiring to the galley.

It was seven o'clock in the morning of the seventeenth of April. Johnston took command of the ship. Over the next two days, the men sent much of the ship's cargo of copper overboard, lightening the *Saladin* and speeding her onwards to the Gulf of St. Lawrence. They lowered Anderson out over the bow to nail a board over the nameplate and to paint the proud copper figurehead white. The *Saladin* had become a ghost of her former self—having lost her captain, part of her cargo, and even her name. With only the apprentice navigator to guide her, the nameless ship set a course northwards with a wild and drunken crew that planned to scuttle her as soon as they made land.

Chapter Eleven

She came out of the fog silently, like a ghost in the night, her tall white sails set and driven by a gale-force wind. Her bow smashed into wave after towering wave as she approached the rocky shoals of Nova Scotia's eastern shore. It was Tuesday, May 21st, 1844.

With a groan that seemed to come from her very soul, the *Saladin* came to a shuddering halt, her belly lodged firmly among the rocks in the shallow water of Harbour Island, near the tiny fishing village of Country Harbour, forty miles west of the Cape of Canso.

She listed to starboard while the high waves from a following sea pummelled her stern and washed over her decks.

"What in hell happened?" yelled Hazelton from the galley floor, where he had been flung when the ship ran aground. His mind was whirling from the impact and from the copious amount of rum coursing through his veins. "Where's Galloway?"

The young navigator had been asleep in his bunk when the ship struck, and, like Hazelton, had been thrown to the floor. He quickly stood up, shaken and bruised, and began a frantic search for his charts. The ship must have come up well short of his projected target, the Strait of Canso. Where were they now? Galloway climbed to the deck, where the wind howled and the waves continued to crash mercilessly. There was no way of obtaining a reading in these conditions. He would have to wait until the weather cleared. But what good would his calculations do now? The ship would pound itself to death on the rocks and break up before the men had sobered up enough to even lower the sails. In their present condition, climbing a pitching mast to perform such a task would be suicidal.

A hand pulled him back below deck. It was Hazelton, the only other seaman sober enough to stand. "Too rough to be up there," he said gruffly to Galloway, shivering in his nightshirt.

"There's no hope, John," said the navigator quietly. "We must abandon ship before she breaks up on the rocks."

"Where are we?" asked Hazelton, his face made haggard by weeks of drinking and little sleep.

"The last sun shot was just west of Halifax six days ago. We must be near Cape Breton, but I can't be sure without a fresh reading."

"I'll go below and wake the men," said Hazelton. "They won't go without their money."

With a gale brewing, the men of the schooner *Billow* had taken shelter on the evening of the twentieth of May. Their captain, William Cunningham, knew that a late shipment of provisions would annoy his Halifax clients, but the weather had been unsettled since they had shipped from Antigonish a few days earlier and showed signs of worsening before it got better; he had therefore decided to put in at Country Harbour and wait out the worst of the storm. By mid-morning of the following day, the weather had settled enough for Cunningham to send a party of men to Harbour Island for freshwater. Despite the gale's weakening grip, the seas were rough, and the men had a hard go of it to the island. When they came back to the *Billow* several hours later, their eyes were wild with excitement: while filling their buckets at the island's spring, they had spotted a large ship with all sails set run aground at the southwestern tip of the island, clearly in distress. The *Billow*'s men had seen signs of activity on deck, but more than that, they could not tell.

Cunningham listened attentively to his excited men's story, then announced, "If there are men aboard, they will be in need of assistance. McNeil—Mahoney—prepare the longboat. We'll try to board her, if the sea will let us."

On board the *Saladin*, an atmosphere of frantic and uncoordinated activity prevailed. The men, still under the influence of whiskey, fought over the money in the ship's hold as though their lives depended on the outcome. Galloway, meanwhile, had found the ship's speaking trumpet and stood at the bowsprit, issuing calls for aid. He had spotted the *Billow* party on the island, and now hailed Captain Cunningham and his men as they made their way toward the stranded vessel. The longboat rose on the crests of the waves and fell into their troughs with a frightening motion, and as they approached the *Saladin*, it seemed several times as though their small boat would overturn. On reaching the ship's side, Cunningham hollered for a rope to be thrown down. Galloway quickly complied. Tying the rope securely around his waist, Cunningham called to the men of the *Saladin* to pull him up. Galloway, Hazelton and Anderson steadied themselves on the pitching bow and pulled with all their strength. With each downward roll of the ship, Cunningham plunged into the icy water, pushing against the side of the ship to keep from being crushed. By the time he was finally hauled on board the ship, the captain was half-drowned and shaking violently from the cold.

"Bill—go get the man some dry clothes!" Galloway yelled at Carr, who had just stumbled up from the galley where he had been sleeping off the effects of a night of drinking.

"Much obliged, young sir," said Cunningham through chattering teeth, holding out a shaking hand. "Captain Cunningham of the schooner *Billow*. Might you be one of the ship's officers?"

"No, no...I was...am...an apprentice, studying navigation," stammered Galloway, suddenly aware that no officers of the *Saladin* remained alive.

"Who might be in charge of this vessel?" asked Cunningham.

Galloway looked at the men around him. "Nobody is, sir. Our captain is dead."

Cunningham looked taken aback. "What about your mate? Someone must be in charge."

"He's dead, too, sir."

"How did they die, pray?" asked Cunningham, wearing a skeptical expression.

Johnston answered for Galloway, his speech slurred.

"'Tis a sad story, to be sure, cap'n. Our master fell ill with the ship's fever a month out of Valparaiso where we was loading up on guano, bound for London. Then the mate took sick with it an' before the week was out, both had gone to meet their Maker." He crossed himself ostentatiously. "Then, as if we hadn't had our fill of bad luck, the second officer falls from the mast and is killed right before our eyes. Left us, poor simple seamen, with no officers nor a captain, and only this lad here to help us with the navigatin'." Johnston laid a fatherly hand on Galloway's shoulder, causing the young man to involuntarily recoil. Johnston's too-familiar, wheedling tone revolted him. Johnston continued, "So as you can see, sir, in our present circumstance, with what's left of the crew taken to drink some time since, what we'd be needing at present is a man such as yourself to take command of this poor ship."

Cunningham looked cautiously sympathetic. "Well, lads, you've gotten yourselves into a pickle. What I don't understand is why no one has taken in the sails yet. Even a fool can see that if the wind shifts, you'll be driven out into deep water and sunk."

Johnston was sheepish. "Beggin' your pardon, sir. But, as I said, with the men being much the worse for drink these past weeks, no one has been in a fit state to do anything around *Saladin*."

Nodding, Cunningham said, "Very well. I will take charge." Gesturing at Johnston and Anderson, he began to give orders.

"You and you—pull my men up over the side and see to it our

boat is well tethered to…what did you call this ship?" he asked Johnston.

"*Saladin*, sir."

"Yes, make fast to *Saladin*. And mind you don't shatter every bone in their bodies on the way up. You were none too gentle on these old bones." He smiled at Galloway.

With considerable effort, the crew was able to pull Cunningham's two men, Laughlin Mahoney and Duncan McNeil, out of their boat in the same manner as they had Cunningham. After several dunkings in the icy water, the two finally stood shivering next to their captain on board the *Saladin*. All six of the ill-fated ship's crew now stood nearby, in various stages of intoxication.

What an ill-favoured pack of dunces, thought Cunningham, surveying them before giving orders. "Now, lads," he said. "Let's see to those sails."

Only Carr and Galloway showed signs of readiness. The four conspirators stood silently, as though they hadn't heard the order.

Cunningham looked surprised. "Come, boys. What ails ye? We'll need all hands to furl those sails. Even the royals are set."

Johnston spoke up. "Sir, as I have said, the crew is much the worse for drink and is not fit for the work."

"You refuse orders when your ship is in peril?" Cunningham was growing angry.

Johnston shrugged. "To be blunt, sir, most of us don't care if the ship sinks where she struck. We've had enough of the sailor's life and propose to quit it as soon as we have recovered ourselves."

Cunningham could not believe his ears. "Well, if you are willing to let such a fine ship go to wrack and ruin, I am not. Come lads," he gestured to his own men. "We will cut down the sails ourselves."

Shooting the mutineers withering looks, Galloway and Carr quickly joined the efforts of the *Billow* men, climbing up the rigging and with great difficulty cutting the wildly flapping sails away from the masts. It was dangerous work, with the ship leaning well to starboard and with her continuous pitching in the rough seas, but the five men finally managed to cut the *Saladin* free from her sheets and decrease the ship's violent rocking.

Returning to the deck where the four drunken men were lolling about listlessly, Cunningham said sarcastically, "Will one of you fine gentlemen show me the cabin? There's still the cargo to see to."

The men snapped suddenly to attention, regarding the captain with fearful eyes.

Jones spoke first, "Well, sir, there's not much but a pile of copper ingots below and the guano, of course."

Cunningham was losing patience. "Well? Don't just stand there jawing—show me it!"

The men were hesitant to let the captain see below decks: all the men's quarters, and especially the captain's cabin, were a shambles. Splintered furniture, broken liquor bottles, piles of clothing, and scattered papers lay everywhere in the aftermath of the men's drunken rampaging. The ship's sextant, quadrant, and chronometer lay on the floor, thrown there with careless disregard. Cunningham and his men were shocked.

"Looks like a hurricane blew through, sir," said McNeil.

The captain was growing suspicious. "Where's your logbook?" he asked Johnston, who reluctantly produced it. The last entry, in Bryerly's hand, was for April twelfth: "Wind SE, cloudy." Then the entries ceased altogether.

"You said your captain and mate died of ship's fever: why are their deaths not noted in the log?"

Johnston could only shrug. "We're just simple seamen, sir. Never learned to read or write."

Cunningham looked at Johnston a long time. He had a growing sense that fever was not the cause of the officers' deaths. He flipped to the front of the book, where the short muster roll was kept.

"'Captain George Fielding, passenger, and son, aged twelve.' You said nothing about passengers. Who are these?"

"A father and son that our captain took on as passengers in Valparaiso. They died also—of the fever."

Cunningham looked at his two men, who shrugged in bewilderment. The *Saladin*'s story was growing stranger by the minute.

Surveying the wreckage in the captain's quarters, Cunningham spotted a large trunk, the only piece of furniture that had not been touched, tucked beneath the bunk. He tried to pull it out, but it would not budge. "Help me with this, lads," he called to his men.

Johnston looked uneasy. "There's nothing in there, sirs. Just some of the late captain's effects, God rest his soul. You'd best leave it where it is. We'll take care of it."

Cunningham straightened up, and grabbed Johnston by the collar. "Look here, you bastard. I'm in charge of this ship now, and I plan to search every inch of her before I'm through. I don't give a damn for your opinions—in fact, your whole story strikes me as highly suspect. My job is to secure the ship and her contents, and you'd best stay out of my way while I'm doing it!"

Johnston backed away.

The *Billow* men finally succeeded in pulling the chest out from under the bunk; using a pocketknife, the captain was able to pry open the lock on the heavy chest. He gasped at its contents: thirteen large bars of Chilean silver gleamed up at him from their wrappings. He guessed their value at ten thousand pounds at least. With urgency in his voice, he gave orders to his men.

"Mahoney, McNeil—get yourselves back to *Billow* at once. Tell them to send a second boat out here immediately—we've got a cargo of silver, copper, and God knows what else to offload before she breaks up. Once you've done that, send for the justice of the peace in Country Harbour—I believe he goes by the name of Archibald. I'll wait here. Oh, and bring me back my pistol."

"Aye, sir." The men left quickly, leaving Cunningham and the conspirators in the cabin.

While he awaited his men's return, the captain set about taking stock of the *Saladin*'s cargo: he made an inventory of all the valuables aboard so that nothing might "disappear" during transport. Once his men returned, he helped them load the silver and much of the copper onto boats bound for the mainland; he even had the foresight to make a second copy of his inventory to send along with each boatload of valuables, lest his own sailors be tempted by the rich cargo. He kept the master list himself.

Cunningham worked the rest of the day and all through the night, readying loads of cargo for his men to remove upon their return. Tirelessly, he continued in his labours all through the next day, keenly aware of the presence of the disgruntled crew. The captain stayed awake two nights, making lists, estimating values, forcing himself to remain conscious. He remained on the *Saladin* thirty-six hours, restoring as much order as he could to the pre-vailing chaos.

The justice of the peace, Charles Archibald, arrived early on the morning of the twenty-third, and it was with considerable relief that Cunningham placed him in charge of both the ship's property and its men, now finally sobering up after many days of inebriation and able to give more coherent answers to Archibald's questions. With the last boatload of valuables well on its way ashore, Cunningham was only too glad to quit the *Saladin* and to continue on his journey to Halifax, where a few days later he made a lengthy deposition to the judge of vice-admiralty, S. G. W. Archibald, about his strange adventure. Acting on the information contained in Cunningham's affidavit, the judge commanded the marshal of the court to seize and hold for safekeeping the goods found on board the *Saladin*; he also authorized the arrest of the six seamen who had acted so suspiciously on the day the captain had boarded their stranded vessel.

The fastest means of travel between Halifax and Country Harbour being by ship, city authorities commissioned the schooner *Fair Rosamond* to transport the seamen back to Halifax to stand trial for suspected piracy. Captain Cunningham was joined on the eastbound schooner by the Honourable Michael Tobin, an underwriter for Lloyd's insurance company, at daybreak on Sunday, May 26, and the ship made ready to sail. On leaving Halifax Harbour, the *Fair Rosamond* encountered unfavourable winds and currents and was forced to return to port to wait out the bad weather.

When the schooner finally reached the wreck of the *Saladin* on the May 31, the six seamen were nowhere to be found. Deeply concerned, Cunningham and Tobin met with the justice of the peace to discuss the case.

"Why did you not arrest them yourself?" Cunningham asked Archibald with barely restrained annoyance.

"The warrant was issued, sir," said the justice of the peace defensively. "We were to apprehend the scoundrels last evening, but when my men arrived at the wreck, the crew had vanished. I spoke with a young lad, Winthrop Cooke, who was out to the ship yesterday morning with a Mr. Burke from Drum Head—said they had been fishing in the area and said a man on the wreck had hailed 'em and asked where a man might buy supplies ashore. Lad said he hadn't heard a word about them being pirates—just assumed they was regular seamen in distress. So he and Burke took two of them ashore to Drum Head, and the men bought plenty of ship's biscuit and salt beef from Grierson, the shopkeeper. Then they rowed 'em back again. The lad showed me the sea chest and straight razor the men gave him as payment; he was right pleased with 'em—he was some shocked when I told him he'd been given a gift from a pirate!" Archibald chuckled at the memory.

Cunningham was clearly distressed. Would all his work securing the ship and its men come to nought?

"They can't have gotten far, Captain," said Tobin, seeing his companion's upset. "Travelling on foot through the woods will make for slow progress." He turned to Archibald. "Have you notified the neighbouring villages of the escape?"

"Indeed, sir, word was out almost before I heard of the escape," said Archibald. "I sent men out to Guysborough, a few miles away, early this morning—the sheriff will be out searching the woods by now."

Twenty miles away from Country Harbour, in the woods of Guysborough County, the Hattie family awoke early in the morning that same day to the sound of a wooden club rapping on the door of their log cabin. A sonorous voice called out: "Open up! This is the deputy sheriff—we need to search your house."

With a start, the four strangers who had been asleep before the kitchen fire jumped up and made for the back door, intent on escape.

Meanwhile, a puzzled Daniel Hattie, still in his nightshirt, opened up the door, through which came bursting three constables armed with pistols and batons. "They're here, sir," one called out to the waiting officer as he and his fellows pinioned the arms of the would-be escapees, who gave themselves up without a struggle. "But there's only four of 'em—I thought Archibald said six men."

Deputy Sheriff Alexander Sinclair of Guysborough looked concerned. "He did say six—one of 'em's got a stump leg. You sure you only took in four?" he asked Daniel Hattie, who stood bewildered in a corner of the kitchen, watching the arrests.

"Yes, sir—four. They told me they were shipwrecked and headed to Halifax to join another crew back to England. What are they wanted for?"

The deputy sheriff looked grim. "Mutiny—murder of a sea captain. Possible theft of valuable cargo."

Hattie's jaw dropped. He had been joined by his wife, dressed in a nightgown and cap and holding their six-month-old baby in her arms. She looked alarmed.

"What is it, Daniel? What do these men want?"

"Begging your pardon, ma'am," Deputy Sheriff Sinclair tipped his hat to Mrs. Hattie. "But you have housed four wanted criminals and we have been sent here to apprehend them."

"Lord have mercy!" cried Mrs. Hattie. The baby began to whimper.

"We'll be on our way, now," said Sinclair. "Wouldn't want to keep an honest woman in the presence of hardened criminals any longer."

As the prisoners shuffled out the door, arms tied firmly behind their backs, Jones smiled apologetically at his hosts.

"I'm very sorry for all this trouble. You are kind folks to have took us in. God bless you."

The Hatties were too stunned to reply.

Later that morning, while changing her baby's cradle clothing, Mrs. Hattie was horrified to discover two silver ingots tucked beneath the sheets. She ran to the woodshed to find her husband, carrying the heavy objects.

"Daniel! Look what they've left behind!"

For the third time that day, Daniel Hattie was too stunned to speak. When he had recovered himself somewhat, he said quietly, "There's no way we can keep them—these are stolen property. Those men are wanted for murder. We'll have to return it to the constables."

Putting down his axe, Hattie loaded the ingots into a haversack and rode out towards Guysborough in the hopes of intercepting the captors, but they had too large a head start. It took him the better part of the day, but he finally reached Guysborough and greatly surprised the officers on duty when he placed the two ingots on their table at the constabulary. After telling the story of their provenance, Hattie prepared to leave, the officers' profound thanks still resounding in his ears.

"Tell the deputy sheriff that we're honest folks and don't go looking for trouble," he said, simply.

On his ride home, he marvelled at the strangeness of the day, and wondered in what ways his family's life might have changed had they kept the illicit silver.

It wasn't long before the two remaining *Saladin* sailors were apprehended by Sinclair and his men, and all six of them delivered back into Justice of the Peace Archibald's custody.

It was with much relief that Cunningham and Tobin watched their prisoners being marched up the gangplank of the *Fair Rosamond* and secured below deck. As they prepared to weigh anchor for Halifax, Archibald called out gaily to Cunningham from the wharf.

"Well, cap'n—the sheriff tells me he received two silver ingots from Daniel Hattie, the man who took our boys in two nights ago. Seems Mrs. Hattie found 'em tucked in among the baby's blankets—Hattie rode all day to Guysborough to see 'em returned. How do you like that?"

Cunningham shook his head in disbelief, then frowned with the remembrance of his hours of painstaking inventorying aboard the *Saladin* a week before. Two more items to account for! He'd let someone else compile the new list.

Chapter Twelve

The approaches to Halifax Harbour are treacherous to the unwary, from the high granite cliffs of Herring Cove Head on the left to the lurking shoals that stretch for half a mile from the weatherbeaten ledge called Thrumcap at the seaward end of McNab's Island. Forty-seven years earlier, observers standing on the cliffs at York Redoubt had watched helplessly as the British frigate *Tribune*, propelled by a brewing gale and a captain unfamiliar with the geography, tore out its belly on these shoals; of the nearly 250 aboard, only 12 survived.

On the clear mid-morning of Monday, the third of June, the *Fair Rosamond* steered clear of the dangerous shoal, keeping to the deepest part of the busy western passage. From beneath the decks of the schooner, the six manacled prisoners could not see McNab's Island, where the bodies of mutinous sailors once swung like suspended scarecrows, their eyes pecked out by crows, their shameful deaths a warning to the many sailors who weighed anchor in the stern little port city of Halifax.

The prisoners could only feel the rhythmic swaying motion of the schooner and observe the increased tempo of footsteps and the familiar sound of sails being furled as the ship drew near its destination. How strange not to be among those men on the decks of the *Fair Rosamond*, each with his own particular task to accomplish toward the smooth running of the ship, tasks which only days ago the manacled men had themselves been performing, albeit haphazardly.

They did not disembark at the busy downtown piers where so many passengers first set foot on shore. Instead, the schooner bore left once it passed the shores of McNab's and continued up the harbour to the provincial penitentiary at Point Pleasant Park, on the Northwest Arm.

Coming down the gangplank with legs stiffened from being chained for three days, the six men were greeted by the large, rectangular, granite building that would be their home while they awaited trial. Even as they were led into their narrow, high-ceilinged cells, the crown was preparing its case against them on charges of piracy and murder. Since the murders had been committed on the high seas, well out of the jurisdiction of any criminal court, a special court was constituted, over which would preside the vice-admiral of the British Navy, along with Chief Justice Haliburton and three other judges of the Supreme Court of Nova Scotia. Meanwhile, inquiries were made in Valparaiso, and a bill of lading showing the full contents of the *Saladin*, along with Captain MacKenzie's agreement with the London-based George and James Brown Company, were requested.

On the day following their arrival in Halifax, Judge Archibald had the six prisoners brought before him and demanded individual accounts of the disappearances of Captain MacKenzie and the other missing men.

In stern, stentorian tones, Archibald advised each of the men as they appeared before him: "You are not required to say anything that might incriminate you—nothing that might make you appear guilty of any wrongdoing."

The judge listened attentively to each man's story, jotting down several glaring discrepancies on a pad of paper. He was certain that the men were lying—quite sure that they had committed murder. He bound them over for trial and returned them to jail.

Once a day, the prisoners at Point Pleasant were taken to the dreary prison yard for fifteen minutes of exercise. As the incarcerated men shambled around the fenced periphery of the enclosure, Galloway approached Carr in an attempt at a private conversation.

"Bill—Bill!" he began in a low voice.

"Leave me be, John. Leave a condemned man be."

"Why should you or I be among the condemned, Bill? We took no part in the mutiny—our consciences are clear!"

From across the yard, Hazelton and Johnston eyed their former shipmates with suspicion. "Would you look at those two schemers?" sneered Hazelton. "John Galloway's a clever bugger. He'll find a way to slip the noose, I'll wager."

Johnston said nothing but plodded on.

"I've got a plan for us, Bill," Galloway continued, across the yard. "If we take responsibility for doing away with Fielding and the boy, the judge will be more willing to believe we had no part in the mutiny. As far as he knows, all six of us are as guilty as sin. We need to separate ourselves from the others." He stole a furtive glance at Johnston and Hazelton, whose stares he could feel burning into his flesh.

Carr stopped short and regarded Galloway with disbelief. "We'll hang yet for the deaths of Fielding and the boy. I threw the poor lad over the railing while he begged for his life." He closed his eyes in pain at the memory.

"We acted in self defense, Bill," Galloway spoke fervently, grasping Carr by the arm. "We were made to do it or our lives were in peril." He paused. "Fielding convinced the others they'd have a share of the spoils when MacKenzie was dead—that was their motive for murder. Ours was self preservation—you know it as well as I." Galloway was urgent now; he could see his argument having an effect on Carr.

"All right, men!" The voice of the warden brought an abrupt end to the discussion. "Back to your cells."

"I have sent word to the attorney general's office that I have something to add to my testimony—your corroboration will infinitely help our case." Galloway spoke hurriedly, as the warden and his men herded their reluctant charges back into the prison. "Can I rely on you, Bill?"

Carr nodded and the two men shook hands.

On the eighth of June, the attorney general, J. W. Johnston, witnessed Galloway's written disclosure of his part in the deaths of the Fieldings. The document ended ominously: "I make the above declaration because I fear to die without disclosing the truth; no man knows how soon I may die." Carr's affidavit ended similarly: "I make this disclosure because I cannot die with such a burden on my mind, and I am perfectly ready to abide by the laws of my country."

The two disclosures drove the final nails into the coffins of Jones, Johnston, Anderson, and Hazelton. For weeks they had maintained that MacKenzie had died some seven to eight weeks earlier, the first officer three days afterwards, and the others shortly thereafter, of fever. Now, perhaps sensing the end was near, the four changed their stories. Johnston was the first to confess, on the tenth of June; Jones, Hazelton, and Anderson were visited by the attorney general the following day and admitted to their parts in the murders. Unable to read or write, Hazelton signed his confession with an "X." Michael Tobin, the Lloyd's agent who witnessed the confessions, assured the court later that the disclosures were made voluntarily, and that they "held out no hope" of reprieve for the prisoners.

The day of arraignment came on the thirteenth of June. In a small courtroom inside Province House, the indictments were read: George Jones, Charles Anderson, William Johnston and John Hazelton were charged with piracy and the murder of Captain MacKenzie. William Carr and John Galloway were charged with the murders of George Fielding and George Fielding, Jr. On the advice of their counsellors, J. B. Uniacke, W. Young and L. O'Connor Doyle, the accused pled "not guilty" to the charges.

Outside the courtroom, a crowd of Haligonians had gathered, eager for a glimpse of the convicted sailors. The *Saladin* story was now a front-page feature of every Nova Scotian newspaper, with coverage of the trial reprinted in the London *Times*. A murder case was exciting enough news in the provincial capital; one that involved piracy on board a treasure ship that had travelled in climes most could only dream about was enough to cause a sensation in the Halifax summer of 1844.

As the prisoners left the courtroom, the throng at the door jostled to get a better view.

"I see 'em! There's the fellow with the wooden peg!"

"That must be Jones—he got a crack in at old MacKenzie."

"They look clean, don't they Joe? I thought they'd be covered in blood."

"Mind your elbow, if you please, sir!"

"They're awfully young, aren't they? The papers didn't mention their ages—why, they can't be more than boys!"

When the prisoners returned for their trial on Thursday, the eighteenth of June, the courtroom was filled to overflowing by newspaper reporters, sensation seekers, the unemployed, and the curious. There was barely enough room for the prisoners once the august assemblage of bewigged judges and black-robed lawyers had taken their places. A raised platform with throne-like chair stood behind the bench: here the commander-in-chief of Her Majesty's ships and vessels in North America would preside. Behind this seat hung a portrait of her sovereign majesty in her round-cheeked youth, a dutifully earnest look upon her small face. Her loyal subjects were about to carry out the law of the queen's domain in her absence.

Although this was to be the trial only of the four indicted for piracy and MacKenzie's murder, all six prisoners had been brought to court. Since their confessions of the previous month, Carr and

Galloway had been the object of frank hatred from their four former shipmates, who took every opportunity of peppering them with threats and insults, outright violence being a virtual impossibility at the prison, where all were manacled. The long wagon ride from the prison to the courthouse had consisted of a long series of epithets, and the ears of Carr and Galloway rang with "Traitors!" and "You'll hang with us yet, dogs!" When they climbed out of the wagon, their clothes were glistening with spittle.

"Move along, you curs!" shouted the bailiff as two of the prisoners stood dazed at the sight of the crowd on the sidewalk in front of the court—a crowd even larger than the one that had gathered on the day of the arraignment.

Hazelton whistled softly. "Didn't know there were so many souls in Halifax," he said to Johnston.

Anderson looked stunned. "All these people come to see us?" he asked a similarly bewildered Jones as they climbed the court steps, blinking in the bright sunshine.

"I reckon so, Charlie. We're the main event."

A hush fell over the raucous audience when a rear door opened and the six manacled prisoners were herded through and into the dock where they sat, conjoined in pairs by iron handcuffs. The animosity between the prisoners, palpable just moments before, was now almost impossible to perceive, the six men too fearful to think of each other.

The presiding vice-admiral, Charles Adam, entered the court after the other officials had taken their places, star of the production that he was. He was resplendent in his dark blue naval uniform decorated with gold epaulettes, stripes, and shiny brass buttons. Seated below the portrait of Victoria, he was the court's presiding authority.

Twelve jurors having been sworn in, the trial was underway. The attorney general rose and began by explaining the unusual nature of this special court that sought to try men from another country for murders committed out of Nova Scotia's jurisdiction and lengthily establishing its precedents, the first from the reign of Henry VIII. Members of the audience grew restless in their seats as the enumeration of precedents continued; several nodded off. The attorney general, sensing the somnolent atmosphere he had created, at length got to the main point: "The evidence upon which the prisoners stand mainly charged is not of an ordinary nature, but it is of a very solemn and weighty character, demanding the grave attention of the jury. Four of the prisoners stand charged with piracy and murder—with felony, committed on the high seas—with making a revolt, and wickedly and feloniously murdering the officers of the *Saladin*—with taking possession of that vessel and a very valuable cargo, consisting of dollars, bars of silver, a quantity of copper, and guano." He underlined the jury's duty in finding the men guilty if a conspiracy among them could be definitively proved. He did not fail to mention the men's free use of liquor and the discrepancies found in their stories by Cunningham and other interrogators. The confessions of Carr and Galloway, who were now seated uncomfortably close to their former shipmates, would be paramount in establishing the guilt of the four accused, as well as their own recent disclosures. The attorney general paused in his speech, then turned to the jury.

"I submit to you that it matters not whose hand struck the blow; they were all leagued against him in one foul conspiracy, and all are equally criminal in the eye of the law."

The attorney general concluded by stressing the importance of this case in establishing a precedent for the punishment of those who committed crimes while in the employ of Her Majesty's merchant marine. "You will bear in mind that this is not a case affecting only our lives or property, but one in which the whole world is interested. Now that Commerce is extending her relations into every portion of the globe, and every sea is whitening with her sails, it is our duty to throw the protection of the law around those who go down to the sea in ships—it is that alone which can give security to the mariner, and guard the interests of the whole civilized world."

The shackled Hazelton, who had been listening to this bit of sententiousness with a sardonic expression, leaned over to Johnston, whispering, "Too bad that some of 'those who go down to the sea in ships' are drunken bastards like MacKenzie."

Johnston nodded, smirking, "They make Commerce out to be a whore, having relations all over the globe, wouldn't you say?"

"The accused will keep silent during court proceedings!" thundered Justice Haliburton, scowling at Hazelton from beneath bushy eyebrows.

Having established the case for the Crown, the attorney general took testimonies from several of the men who had boarded the wreck of the *Saladin* in Country Harbour the previous month. He then took his seat.

A clearly agitated Johnston, listening impatiently to the attorney general's lengthy rhetoric, now jumped to his feet, dragging Hazelton with him. "Please your Honour," he exclaimed, "I wish to be allowed to address the court."

Haliburton scowled again. "Mr. Johnston! That is the duty of your counsel."

"But I wish to be allowed to speak in my own defense, your Honour," said Johnston fervently. "I wish to change my plea."

A murmur of excitement passed through the audience.

"Mr. Johnston, this is highly irregular."

"Please, your Honours…"

Beckoning to the Crown prosecutor and the prisoners' attorneys, Justice Haliburton conferred briefly with them, then cleared his throat magisterially.

"Prisoner Johnston, you have been granted permission to address the court in your own defense."

"Thank you, Mr. Justice." Johnston bowed to Haliburton, who

nodded curtly in reply. The bailiff removed the manacles joining Johnston to Hazelton, who sat down again. From his place in the prisoners' box, Johnston removed a grimy piece of paper from his pocket and unfolded it carefully, beginning to read. "Gentlemen of the jury, I wish it to be recorded that I am changing my plea from 'not guilty' to 'guilty.' In so doing, I am throwing myself upon your clemency in light of certain mitigating circumstances related to my case. Your Honour, Alexander MacKenzie was the most severe and dissatisfied master I ever sailed under, and my fellow prisoners will vouch for the fact. Had it not been for the plausible reasoning and persuasiveness of that fiend in human shape, Captain Fielding, who, in a thoughtless and unlucky moment induced me to become a pirate and murderer of my comrades, then I would have endured the harsh treatment I received from Captain MacKenzie in the hopes of seeing again my poor mother and father back home in Liverpool. I derive great satisfaction from knowing I helped save the lives of William Carr and John Galloway, by forcibly persuading Fielding not to kill them and by throwing overboard the weapons he would have used against them."

With a decisive nod, Johnston bowed again to Justice Haliburton and the assembled before taking his seat once more.

The lawyers for the other prisoners were the next to speak, urging the jurors to dismiss from their minds the confessions made by Carr and Galloway, and to view the mutiny on board the *Saladin* as a dreadful tragedy in which four young seamen were led astray by the machinations of the "fiend in human shape," Captain Fielding. Only fear for their lives could have forced the sailors to commit such despicable acts, argued the defense attorneys; avarice, they loftily pronounced, was not a "sailor-like vice." They further stressed MacKenzie's harsh and unapproachable nature and reminded the jury of Jones' attempted warning to the captain of the brewing plot against his life, and the captain's curt dismissal. Jones, his lawyers argued, had been repeatedly threatened by Fielding, and wished not to take part in the crimes, facts that they hoped the jury might consider mitigating circumstances. Hazelton's lawyer said that the same circumstances also applied to his client. Even the audience could tell that the lawyers for the defence spoke only half-heartedly. The prisoners' own confessions of guilt made an acquittal impossible, and Chief Justice Haliburton was quick to point out that had the four conspirators felt in real danger, they could have alerted the mate and their other victims to their plight, overpowering Fielding by sheer numbers. Like the attorney general, Mr. Justice Haliburton stressed the broader societal ramifications of mutiny: "Mariners are in an especial manner bound to protect the life of the master with whom they sail," an admonition that aroused a murmur of assent from the citizens in attendance; Halifax had always been intimately tied to the sea, both through its long association with the British navy and by the number of merchant ships that regularly docked along its shorefront and filled its warehouses with imported goods. For a crew member to murder his ship's master seemed to the average Haligonian a far more serious matter than the murder of an ordinary civilian. If captains and their officers were struck down, who would enlist in the navy and merchant marine, and how would towns like Halifax survive?

The jury of Halifax men returned its verdict within a quarter of an hour: All four prisoners were found guilty.

Chapter Thirteen

The jury's unanimous verdict struck terror to the hearts of William Carr and John Galloway, who were to be tried separately for the killings of George Fielding and his son. While their former shipmates fell into an exhausted sleep upon being returned to prison, Carr and Galloway lay awake most of the night in their stifling cell, their fates yet to be decided. From the smalll, barred opening in the granite wall high above their heads, the two men could hear crickets chirping, the slow lap of the waves on the gravelly shore.

"You awake, Bill?"

Carr sighed heavily. "What is it, John?"

"We had no choice, did we, Bill? We had to kill that boy, didn't we?" There was a pleading note in the younger man's voice that made Carr infinitely sad. He did not reply. In truth, the image of the twelve-year-old's face, the grip of his small hands on Carr's arm, perpetually haunted the cook's days and nights.

The court reconvened on the nineteenth of July at Province House with some of the same jurors as had passed sentence on their crewmates the day before. It was apparent from the beginning that the attorney general believed that the two men had committed murder under mitigating circumstances, reiterating that their victim, Fielding, had been the mastermind behind the *Saladin* mutiny, had convinced members of the crew to kill on his orders, and was, in fact, planning for the disposal of the two men on trial. The attorney general allowed that Carr and Galloway had both been asleep at the time of the mutiny. Although they had initially given false statements to the court of admiralty, they later made disclosures that helped ascertain the four conspirators' guilt. But they had shared in the initial division of the money after MacKenzie's murder, and unless they had been under duress when they helped throw Fielding overboard, they were, indeed, guilty.

That Carr and Galloway were, in fact, under duress at the time of Fielding's death was the main thrust of defence attorney J. B. Uniacke's argument; he stated that the circumstances surrounding Fielding's death were such "as would legally justify the act in the eyes of a humane British jury." Turning his gaze for a moment on the attorney general as if what he was about to say was intended primarily for him, Uniacke continued, "No crime can be perpetrated unless the actors are acting voluntarily in its commission: in all criminal cases, the law requires free agency, and sanctions deeds of violence necessary for self-preservation. My clients were involuntary actors in a scene at which their feelings revolted." Prisoner Johnston, said Uniacke, had warned the two that death awaited them when the *Saladin* reached land if Fielding lived. Under threat from all sides, could his clients have acted differently? Did they have a choice in the matter? Was it any wonder that it was considered necessary to purge the *Saladin* of its resident demon? Uniacke allowed his impressive rhetoric to carry him along for several more minutes. "It is a principle of law, that when a man destroys even his own life under particular circumstances, where he is driven to it by fear or desperation, he must be considered guiltless."

Chief Justice Haliburton had heard enough. "Mr. Uniacke, was not Captain Fielding as much under the protection of the law when he was thrown overboard as the prisoners you represent? Do you suggest to this jury that the prisoners are to be considered innocent of the crime of murder simply because Fielding had also committed murder?"

Uniacke looked flustered, "Why, sir—I had not thought…"

Haliburton continued, "Indeed, sir, Captain Fielding was entitled to the same protections under the law as his accused killers. I am surprised to hear the learned counsel for the prisoners state to the jury for law that which the court cannot admit to be such."

Uniacke looked crestfallen, but knew better than to answer back.

Carr shivered as though a cold breeze had passed through the courtroom.

The case against the two men for the murder of George Fielding, Jr., covered the same territory as in the captain's case. The attorney general advised the jury that the same logic that had motivated the two men to throw overboard a dangerous killer like Fielding could not be similarly applied in the killing of a twelve-year-old boy. That they were afraid the boy might testify against them in a later trial could not justify the crime they committed. With that statement, the Crown rested its case.

Uniacke reiterated the threats against his clients' lives issued by the four conspirators as sufficient motive for George's killing. "The two acts of destroying father and son are in reality one," he said. "They were compelled to perform them to save themselves."

The Chief Justice questioned Uniacke's interpretation of the boy's killing, adding that he doubted that this was a case of legitimate self defense.

After two hours of deliberation, the jury returned with a verdict of not guilty. The triumphant Uniacke had proven his case.

Galloway jumped to his feet and shook his attorney's hand warmly. Carr could not believe that he had heard the words "not guilty." He heard Galloway speaking to him somewhere above the tumult in the crowd: "We're free, Bill—thank God we're free!" Carr closed his eyes again the tears that were welling up, but all he could see was George's terrified face as he plunged into the ocean. At that moment, Carr would have gladly traded places with the mutineers, whose worldly concerns were almost over.

On Saturday, the twentieth of July, the court convened for the last time, to sentence Anderson, Jones, Johnston, and Hazelton. Since their conviction two days earlier, none of the four had eaten or slept: many in the gallery of the court remarked how gaunt and haggard they looked. The attorney general moved that the charge of piracy be dropped; he did not wish to add insult to injury by exposing the bodies of the condemned men to rot in chains on the gallows, the traditional punishment for pirates.

In solemn tones, the Chief Justice chastised the four for the terrible crimes they had committed; like a fire-and-brimstone clergyman, he exhorted his rapt congregation to heed the moral lesson to be taken from the sorry affair. "Let each and all of the numerous audience that now contemplate your sad condition remember, that often it is only the first step to crime that can be resisted. These unhappy victims are hurried without warning into the presence of their Maker—you have had, and will still have, time to make your peace with God. You will still have the aid of pious clergymen to prepare your spirits for their final departure." The Chief Justice paused for dramatic effect. "Nothing remains for me but to pronounce the awful sentence of the law—that you, George Jones—you, John Hazelton—you, William Johnston—and you, Charles Gustavus Anderson, be taken to the place from whence you came, and thence to the place of execution, and there to be hanged by the neck till you are dead; and may God have mercy on your souls."

Prisoner Johnston, who had risen slowly to his feet as the judge was speaking, dragging his handcuffed partner Jones with him, requested permission to speak. A ripple of spirited whispers arose from the gallery. The Chief Justice looked irritated with this intrusion into the smooth formalities of the court.

"Prisoner Johnston—you have had your chance to speak. Surely nothing remains to be said."

"You are wrong, your honour," answered Johnston in a quavering voice. "I wish it to be recorded that I had no part in the killing of the boy. I wasn't raised to harm a child, and I don't wish the boy's death to rest on the shoulders of my family. That's all, your honour."

Johnston and Jones took their seat.

"Very well, prisoner Johnston, very well," said the Chief Justice, glad to have the interruption over with. "Guard! Remove the prisoners—this court is adjourned."

As they shuffled out, Hazelton leaned anxiously over to Johnston. "They didn't say when, Bill. They didn't tell us the day."

"They never do, Johnny," said Johnston. "And do you really want to know it?"

The crowd that stood outside the courtroom in the bright July sun grew silent as the four condemned men were led past them. Several noticed the tears on Anderson's drawn face, the men's slumped, defeated shoulders. Though justice had to be done, to many of the more sympathetic members of the crowd, it all seemed a terrible waste.

"Hurrah! MacKenzie is avenged!" a lone voice cried out.

"Death to pirates!" shouted another.

"Quiet, you fools!" rebuked a third. "Isn't it enough they's to be hanged?"

Chapter Fourteen

In the sweltering prison on the Northwest Arm, the four men awaited the day of their deaths. Anderson whittled steadily on whatever material came within his grasp—when no wood was forthcoming, he whittled a tiny Easter basket from a peach pit he found in a corner of his cell. The warden, taking pity on his foreign prisoner, allowed Anderson the privilege of keeping his pocket knife. The high slits in the granite that passed for windows allowed in little light and not even a glimpse of the ocean, which they could only hear slopping quietly on the pebbly shore at night. The men found that sound a greater comfort than the daily visits they received from clergymen who constantly inquired about the health of their souls. After the departure of an especially solicitous Roman Catholic priest one afternoon, Johnston couldn't help but quip to his cellmate Jones, "I don't know about you, George, but with all the attention it's gotten since we've been here, my soul's never been better; it's the rest of me that needs help now!"

Outside the confines of the prison, all of Halifax awaited the announcement of the day of execution. At the pubs and stews of Barrack Street that lined the base of Citadel Hill, sailors shook their heads in sympathy with the doomed men, cursing men like Alexander MacKenzie who harassed their crews into desperate actions, while prostitutes stroked their hair and nodded in agreement. Many a Barrack Street lady had once saved young men like the *Saladin* sailors from the press gangs, hauling them off the unsafe streets into their establishments just ahead of the British recruiting officers.

In the more fashionable establishments of Tower Road and Inglis Street, the well-heeled captains of trading vessels and British navy brass heaved a sigh of relief when they read the news of the pirates' convictions over their morning tea and toast. What was the world coming to, they puffed indignantly, when the scum of Liverpool and Newcastle could dream of taking over a ship loaded with valuables, heaving the master overboard like so much ballast? Hanging was too good for them—and Halifax was already overrun with corrupt and godless seamen, to be sure.

When the date of execution finally appeared on the front page of the *Novascotian*, Halifax's sailors and sea captains alike marked Tuesday, the thirtieth of July, on their calendars, for very different reasons: some would mourn the passing of a misled crew, while others would rejoice in the public death of convicted mutineers.

In all the excitement over the hangings, few noticed the small item that appeared in the back pages of the *Novascotian* relating to the ship that had brought the four sailors to their sad fate in Halifax. The *Saladin*, stripped of her cargo, sails and tackle, had broken up and sunk where she lay off the shores of Harbour Island, a place that came to be known as Saladin Point.

The scaffold was erected upon a grassy knoll on the South Common, just opposite the Catholic Cemetery where a little chapel, built in a day, stood at the top of a hill. The construction of the scaffold drew a crowd of spectators, morbidly eager to witness its subsequent operation. An upright post was situated at each end of the platform on which the prisoners were to stand. A wooden beam ran the length of the platform and rested of the tops of the posts; four nooses hung from this beam. Built into the floor of the platform were four trap-doors, called drops, each held in place by a wooden button. All four buttons were attached to a single long cord, a tug on which released all four drops simultaneously.

The day of execution arrived. The prisoners were awoken by the warden at sunrise and informed that this was to be their final day. Anderson burst into tears; Jones tried to comfort him. "There, there, Charlie," he spoke softly. "It'll soon be over." The prisoners bathed and were given a fresh set of clothes to wear. They ate a hearty breakfast of fried eggs and corned beef hash, their final meal.

Two closed carriages were used to transport the condemned the three-and-a-half mile distance from the penitentiary to the scaffold, where a crowd of several thousand waited patiently. Early in the morning, a company of the Fifty-second Foot Guards formed a protective circle around the scaffold to keep spectators at a proper distance.

At about ten o'clock, a small procession made its way down Tower Road: the sheriff in his gig led the group, then came the ominous horse-drawn carriages containing the doomed men, accompanied by three Catholic priests and an Anglican minister. On each side of the two carriages marched an armed guard, their fixed bayonets gleaming in the sun.

Billy Isnor, who had travelled all night with his family from Lunenburg in his father's oxcart, sat balanced on a headstone in the cemetery across the street from where the hangings would take place, eating one of his mother's biscuits with molasses, his favorite meal. The family had arrived early so as to get the best view, which they believed would prove edifying to their sons, Billy, age eight, and his brother Harold, six. Their father, a blacksmith of German extraction, hoped that his boys would join the navy as soon as they were old enough, and have the chance to see the world instead of the black inside of a forge. The navy, Isnor knew, imposed strict discipline: what better way to illustrate this fact than at a public hanging?

"Billy!" called his mother, seated on a picnic blanket she had spread out between two large stone crosses. "Get off that headstone! The Lord punishes those who make light of the dead."

"Hush, Matilda," said her husband. "The lad means no harm—besides, this is a Popish churchyard. I've never given a damn for what a Catholic thought."

"Good heavens, William! We aren't heathens, are we?—what will people think? Get off that stone this instant, Billy!"

The boy reluctantly slid down off his sandstone perch.

"When will they get here, mamma?" asked Harold, tired of waiting.

"Soon enough, my dear," replied his mother, smoothing out his tousled hair.

Walking a few yards down South Street and looking down Tower Road along with the thousand other spectators, Billy spotted the procession arriving. He ran back to the cemetery:

"They're coming! They're coming!"

The boy was suitably impressed by the display of military prowess that suffused the event. He shuddered, though, to look at the gallows, the place his parents often warned him that bad boys would end their careers if they did not mend their ways.

He watched intently as the prisoners climbed out of their hearse-like carriages, pale and debilitated by their stay in prison. His father put an arm around his shoulder as the prisoners mounted the scaffold and the nooses were placed around their necks. The crowd was almost completely silent; Billy could even hear the mumbling of the black-robed priests, saying the rosary with Jones and Hazelton, the Catholic prisoners. Anderson alone seemed strangely unfazed by his fate, gazing steadily above the heads of the spectators and out to sea, the place he loved best. "I'm coming home," he murmured in his own language. "I'm coming home."

Before the hoods were placed over their heads, discreetly covering the facial contortions they would undergo in their death struggle, the prisoners shook hands. Jones kissed each of his condemned colleagues affectionately on the cheek, whispering "Goodbye, lad," to each. Then he addressed the spectators in a final leave-taking.

"My name is George Jones. I am an Irishman from County Clare, where my parents still live. They will grieve to hear the news of my death. I am deeply sorry for what I have done and I pray that God will have mercy on my soul and see fit to grant me pardon."

The black hoods were pulled over their heads, and the clergymen descended the scaffold, kneeling in prayer next to four open coffins. A drum roll began from somewhere behind the scaffold; when it stopped, the executioner pulled the cord, releasing the drops. The men struggled for a moment, and were still. Billy opened his mouth to scream, but no sound came out. His father drew the boy to him and held him tightly in his arms. Looking up, Billy saw tears in his father's eyes. He had not known that a man could cry.

The Isnor family, like most of the spectators, stood transfixed at the sight of the four lifeless bodies swaying gently in the summer breeze. It was Mrs. Isnor who spoke first.

"Well—that's that, William. You've had your wish—the boys saw four lives taken. Now can we please return home? The cow'll need milking and I have a mess of mending to do."

As they left the South Common, Billy and Harold could not help looking back at the scaffold and its sad prey. They were almost to Citadel Hill in the plodding oxcart before they finally lost sight of the four bobbing heads. It was a sight they would tell their grandchildren about.

Afterword

The bodies of the four men were cut down after forty-five minutes; Hazelton and Jones were buried in the Catholic Cemetery across the street and Johnston and Anderson were laid to rest in unmarked paupers' graves. Anderson's skull was later exhumed and used by Dalhousie Medical School as a teaching tool for its anatomy classes.

What became of John Galloway and William Carr, the two acquitted *Saladin* sailors?

According to local lore, Carr settled in Digby, Nova Scotia and lived a long and respectable life. He was known for his devout churchgoing, as well as his peculiar habit of getting around at a brisk trot, perhaps as a result of his days on the *Saladin* when for several weeks he had had to keep one step ahead of death. Every April the thirteenth, the anniversary of the mutiny, he drowned his sorrows in liquor.

Galloway simply disappeared.

A legend persists in Halifax that if you find yourself awake early on the morning of the thirteenth of July, you may witness the same ghostly procession of carriages and foot soldiers through the city streets, heading towards the fatal knoll where the story of the *Saladin* finally ended.

The Ballad of George Jones
traditional

Good people all, come listen to my melancholy tale,
My dying declaration which I have pen'd in jail.
My present situation may to all a warning be,
And a caution to all seamen to beware of mutiny.

George Jones is my name, I am from the county Clare,
I quit my aged parents and left them living there.
I being inclined for roving, at home I would not stay,
And much against my parents' will I shipped and went to sea.

My last ship was the *Saladin*, I shudder at her name,
I joined her in Valparaiso on the Spanish Main.
I shipped as cabin steward which proved a fatal day,
A demon came aboard of her which led us four astray.

I agreed to work my passage, the sip being homeward bound,
With copper ore and silver and over thousand pounds;
Likewise two cabin passengers on board of her did come,
The one was Captain Fielding, the other was his son.

He did upbraid our captain before we were long at sea,
And one by one seduced us into a mutiny;
The tempting prize did tempt his eyes, he kept it well in view,
And by his consummate art he's destroyed us all but two.

On the fourteenth night of April I am sorry to relate,
We began his desperate enterprise—at first we killed the mate;
Next we killed the carpenter, and overboard him threw,
Our captain next was put to death with three more of the crew.

The watch were in their hammocks when the work of death begun,
The watch we called, as they came up we killed them one by one;
These poor unhappy victims lay in their beds asleep,
We called them up and murdered them, and hove them in the deep.

There were two more remaining still below and unprepared,
The hand of God protected them that both their lives were spared;
By them we're brought to justice and both of them are free.
They had no hand in Fielding's plan, nor his conspiracy.

An oath was next administered to the remainder of the crew,
And like a band of brothers we were sworn to be true.
This was on a Sunday morning when the bloody deed was done,
When Fielding brought the Bible and sword us every one.

The firearms and weapons all we threw into the sea,
He said he'd steer for Newfoundland, to which we did agree,
And secret all our treasure there in some secluded place;
If it was not for his treachery that might have been the case.

We found with Captain Fielding (for which he lost his life)
A brace of loaded pistols, likewise a carving-knife;
We suspected him for treachery which did enrage the crew;
He was seized by Carr and Galloway and overboard was threw.

His son exclaimed for mercy, as being left alone,
But his entreaties were soon cut off, no mercy there shown.
We served him like his father was who met a water grave,
So we buried son and father beneath the briny wave.

Next it was agreed upon before the wind to keep,
We had the world before us then, and on the trackless deep;
We mostly kept before the wind as we could do no more,
And on the twenty-eight of May we were shipwrecked on the shore.

We were all apprehended, and into prison cast,
Tried and found guilty, and sentence on us passed,
Four of us being condemned and sentenced for to die,
And the day of execution was the thirtieth of July.

Come, all you pious Christians, who God is pleased to spare,
I hope you will remember us in your pious prayer;
Make appeals to God for us, for our departing souls.
I hope you will remember us when we depart and mould.

Likewise the pious clergymen, who for our souls did pray,
Who watched and prayed along with us, whilst we in prison lay;
May God reward them for their pains, they really did their best;
They offered holy sacrifice to God to grant us rest.

And may the God of mercy, who shed His blood so free,
Who died up on the holy cross all sinners to set free.
We humbly ask His pardon for the gross offence we gave,
May He have mercy on our souls when we descend the grave.

We were conveyed from prison, unto the gallows high,
Ascended on the scaffold, whereon we were to die.
Farewell, my loving countrymen, I bid this world adieu,
I hope this will a warning be to one and all of you.

They were placed upon the fatal drop, their coffins beneath their feet,
And their Clergy were preparing them, their Maker for to meet;
They prayed sincere for mercy, whilst they humbly smote their breast,
They were launched into eternity, and may God grant them rest.

"George Jones" is one of three traditional ballads about
the *Saladin* collected by Helen Creighton
and included in her 1932 book
Songs and Ballads from Nova Scotia
(Toronto: J. M. Dent & Sons Limited).

Want to read more about real-life pirates from Nova Scotia's nautical past?

In the early 1800s, on a schooner somewhere between Britain and
Quebec, Ned Jordan turned from passenger to pirate.
Read all about the events leading up to the well-publicized
Halifax trial and hanging of the infamous pirate Ned Jordan
in a new book by Elizabeth Peirce, forthcoming in October 2007
from Nimbus Publishing.

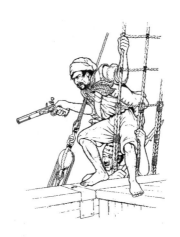